Holidays at Brew by Brewer

The Brewer Brothers

Elsie James

Published by Elsie James, 2023.

Table of Contents

Spooked, Chapter One: Shawn

It's like my body knew the moment I stepped onto Misty Mountain soil and it went into high alert. I've only been back here a few hours and my stomach is wound into tight knots. My hands are clammy, the muscles in my throat are perpetually clenched. I suppose it's some kind of muscle-memory-trauma-response. In fact, I'm sure of it.

My little sister Stella is literally the only person in the world who could get me back to Misty Mountain after all that's happened. Not that I'm ever too far from it no matter how far I go, this town hangs over me like a shadow even when I'm at home in the city.

There's a constant reel of memories that play in my mind on a loop. Normally I can keep them at bay, but the way they come to life against the backdrop of my small hometown is downright spooky.

"Sir, are you checking in?" The woman behind the counter at the hotel at Brew by Brewer looks up at me. "Sir, your name please."

I snap my attention back to her. "Sorry, it's Shawn Willman. I have two adjoining rooms booked, please."

"Not a problem, I'll need to see some identification and the card you used to make the reservation. Also, will your guest need a key?"

I hesitate. "Yeah, I suppose she will." I take a step away from the counter and then lean back in. "You know what, why don't you leave her key here and she can pick it up when she arrives. Please hold it for Kaylee Allen."

Saying her name aloud for the first time feels odd and unnatural. I look at the woman's face to see if she registered anything out of the ordinary in my tone. But she hardly looks up from her keyboard at all.

"Sure thing. Give me a moment and I'll have that all squared away for you." The woman disappears behind the counter.

I look around and take in the sights of the hotel. They've done an impressive job getting this place ready for Halloween. Not that it needed a ton of work. The Brewer family has converted the ancient poor farm in our town into a luxury resort, but they've kept all its original, old-world, charm.

Now, ancient chandeliers, old oak carved doors, and brass fixtures are topped with faux spider webs. A man dressed as a werewolf walks casually through the lobby. Leave it to my little sister to hold a wedding that lasts not one but three days and ends on Halloween.

It isn't usually a romantic holiday. But in Stella's case, the dude she's marrying, Spencer Brewer, is pretty sinister, so I guess it makes sense.

Spencer Brewer has been an unwelcome part of my life for the last six years since he knocked my sister up. I'll give it to the guy, he made a cute kid, my niece is to die for. But that's the only thing he has going for him as far as I can tell.

Well, that and the fact that his family isn't too bad either. I went to school with the Brewers who live here in Misty Mountain, and they're all right, nothing like their cousin Spencer. They own this property and offered it up free of charge for the ceremony.

"Uncle Shawn!" The voice of my adorable niece McKenna sounds behind me and I turn to see her running toward me, arms open, and a gapped tooth smile on her face.

"Kenna," my heart skips a beat.

When I see her, all is right in my world, if only for a minute. When I scoop down and pick her up, I feel full again. McKenna seems to be the only thing that fills the gaping hole inside me.

McKenna and I have been video chatting on our usual schedule, but I feel a pang of sadness stab at my stomach when I realize she's so much bigger than the last time I saw her. "I think you grew a whole foot. What are you, like twenty-five now?"

"Uncle Shawn, I'm still six," she giggles and I put her down.

"If it isn't my big brother, it's good to see you." My sister Stella hugs me.

She of all people understands what it's costing me to be back here for the weekend. I can't help but think of how many times she's come through for me in the last five years and I feel a pang of guilt stab at me for living so far away.

"It's the bride herself, how are you doing with all of this? They certainly did good by your spooky wedding theme. Which is fitting given you're marrying Spencer." I lower my voice and lean in toward my sister, staying out of my niece's earshot. "Are you sure you want to go through with this?" I know I shouldn't ask but I'm the only person who can get away with it.

"Stop it," Stella shakes her head at me. "I'm already in the situation, all you can do now is support me. Besides, a Halloween-themed wedding is worth it if only to see my big brother in an array of costumes... and to hang out with your mysterious new girlfriend. I literally can't wait to meet her!"

Me neither. I wonder what she'll be like. I wonder if I can pull this off.

"She, uh... Kaylee had to fly in late. She had a work thing. But she'll be here." I swallow back my nerves.

McKenna hops up and down, her dark hair in pigtails. "I've got so many costumes! I have a princess one, a zombie, and..." McKenna covers her mouth to control her fits of giggles. "And Uncle Shawn you aren't going to guess... a cat costume! With a tail!"

"That is so cool, I can't wait to see them," I tell her.

As I chat with my sister and niece I have to admit that being in Misty Mountain feels better than I thought it would. I'd forgotten about the small-town charm. The way people say hello to you when they pass. The simple luxury of inhaling clean, mountain air and the way my niece lights up when I talk to her.

"What's up, Big Will?" Spencer's voice is like nails on a chalkboard and it punctures my moment of bliss. Spencer talks four decibels above everyone else in the lobby. He stands uncomfortably close to me and claps me on the back with unnecessary force. His white-blond hair is thinner than the last time I saw him, and his eyebrows are nonexistent.

"Hello, Spencer. Just a reminder that literally no one calls me that." I try to keep my face from pinching into tight lines. I glance at my sister and for her sake, I muster up as much good-willed enthusiasm as I can. "Congratulations."

Spencer's mouth turns down at the corners. "I figured it was time I made it official with the old ball and chain. I mean, I already put a baby in her, I'm already stuck. Plus she's got a decent job for now, so if she wants to be a sugar momma for life, I'm here for it."

Good-willed enthusiasm, over. All I can think to respond with is *you son of a bitch*. But I look at my niece McKenna and keep myself together. "Come on now, I'm sure you're looking forward to making your family official."

But Spencer is already engrossed in some kind of video on his phone, so much so that he doesn't even seem to hear me. So much so, that when my niece reaches for her dad's hand, he doesn't flinch except to pull it away.

"Spencer." My tone is a thinly veiled threat.

He chuckles. "It's cats with bread on their heads, paired with women with big tits... Classic." Spencer holds up the video in my direction. "Hey man, I'm gonna ditch these broads in a bit and get drunk to get through this weekend. You down?"

"Absolutely not. Unbelievable." I turn my head away from him, fury bubbling in my stomach. My eyes flick to Stella, but she's avoiding my stare. I know my sister well enough to say with confidence that it isn't an accident, but I lean in toward her anyway. "You're okay with this? You're voluntarily marrying... this?"

But Stella only rolls her eyes with a shrug and waves me off as McKenna rattles on excitedly about her costumes. For being one of the smartest people I know, Stella isn't making good choices right now and it makes me sick.

My list of grievances with Spencer is long and detailed. But all of them start and end with the way he disrespects my sister and takes my niece for granted. The woman behind the desk finally returns with my room key and I breathe out with relief. At least I have the option of taking myself out of the situation before I say something I'll regret.

"Here you are, we'll leave this key for your guest. Give us a call at the front desk if you need anything." The woman hands over my room key along with a map of the seventy-four-acre property.

"Thanks." I turn to my sister. "I'm gonna head up to my room."

"Okay, don't forget, the rehearsal dinner is tonight. It's full costume required and it'll be so much fun. I know Mom and Dad are more than ready to see you. Our wedding planner Lauren has pulled out all the stops. This weekend should be downright scary," Stella says.

My eyes flash to Spencer. "Now that I can believe. Kenna, come here girl, give Uncle Shawn a hug. I can't wait to see your cool costume in a little bit."

"Later Big Will," Spencer calls over his shoulder without bothering to look up from his phone.

I all but fly up the stairs to my room, more than ready to put some space between Spencer and me. As hard as I try, I can't see what my sister sees in that guy. Her choosing him is not something I'll ever understand.

When I step inside my hotel room, I'm relieved to see that there is in fact an adjoining door. It's an essential piece to the puzzle of this wedding weekend. The last thing I want to do is make her uncomfortable. I crack it open and step through into what will be

Kaylee's room. It's weird to think that at any moment, Kaylee Allen, who has been nothing more than a name on a piece of paper, will be here in person.

My assistant helped me come up with three couple's costumes for this weekend. She's packaged each into its own bag with all the parts and labeled them for me. Best of all, she didn't ask any questions, she's good like that. She's more than happy to give me my space and I dread the day she retires.

I find the three bags with Kaylee's name on them and lay them on her bed. Then I step out and close the adjoining door. I plop onto my own bed and attempt to fire through some work emails. But it isn't any use, I can't focus. Rather, I can't believe this is what I've been reduced to, hiring a date for my sister's wedding.

It's odd, but I couldn't see any other options. So I was as careful with the selection process as possible. I needed someone who could meet all of my specifications. It'd be nice if she was friendly, or at least not unpleasant. It'd be even better if she was attractive, but I thought I might be pushing my luck.

The list of things I'd prefer stretched on and on. But when it came down to writing the advertisement, I could only think of five things that actually mattered.

Needed: Wedding Date/ Fake Girlfriend

1. *No husband or boyfriend. Please no jealous psychos showing up.*
2. *No kids. In my experience, adding a child to anything makes it immediately complicated.*
3. *No breaking character. We need to look like a couple madly in love for the duration of the three-day event. Must cling to our agreed-upon backstory.*
4. *Couples costumes are required for events, I will provide them.*
5. *No sex or intimacy of any kind required. I'm not a creep.*

When I saw it in black and white, it seemed like a lot to ask, so I made sure to offer an astronomical amount of cash. It only made sense to exchange something I have too much of for something I don't have at all... and it worked.

I received hundreds of replies. Immediately I went to work, weeding out the spam and having my assistant help pair down the pile. When I found Kaylee's application, something in her simple, kind responses drew me to her. She seemed down to earth. Normal. Drama-free. It was a process to find her, but it was better than the alternative of showing up back in Misty Mountain alone.

It was worth the effort to avoid the pitying looks and questions. Everyone thinks they know how long you should grieve. But this, what I'm doing, isn't grief, I'm past that. This is an acknowledgment of the fact that I am meant to be alone.

I tried love once, and it was a supreme effort that took me to hell and back. In the end, it wasn't meant to be. I've made my peace with that, but it seems no one else has. Ever since it happened, my parents worry about me. My sister worries about me. My old friends worry, but I don't. I'm okay on my own.

As the afternoon winds on, my nerves start to get the better of me. Kaylee and I have emailed back and forth, but it's been all business. It'd be nice to at least meet this woman for more than five minutes before we have to convince people that we are desperately in love.

I wonder if she's here yet. I don't hear anything next door. I look at the clock and bide my time, taking a shower, and unzipping the bag labeled, *Shawn Outfit #1*. On top of the outfit, there's a note in my assistant's old-lady penmanship.

Sorry, this is all they had last minute. The other two are better. Enjoy, Margie

When I peer inside, at first I have no idea what I'm even looking at. It looks like some kind of blue suit made from plastic. It's complete with a white button-down shirt, pink suspenders, and a matching pink bowtie. It isn't until I pull out the plastic wig that I realize my lovely assistant has made me a Ken doll. I chuckle to myself as I pull it on. As if this day isn't weird enough, I might as well be the least sexy man in America.

When the clock hits four, I only have an hour until my sister's rehearsal dinner and I pull out my phone and punch in a text to Kaylee.

Me: *Hello, This is Shawn Willman. I'd like to meet if you are up for it.*

Before she can respond, my stomach bubbles and anxiety rises in my throat. I punch out another text.

Me: *Although of course you aren't required to spend any additional time with me per our contract, so if you are not interested that's okay too.*

I am completely off my game. My divorce was five years ago at this point and admittedly, I haven't dated much since then, but I didn't think I was this bad. Three minutes pass and I start to worry whether she's come at all. Shaking my head at myself, I punch out a third message.

Me: *I will be outside of your door when it's time to go per our agreement.*

Nerves prickle on the back of my neck. What if I've completely misread the situation? What if she's miserable or if our connection is totally unrealistic? If my family sees right through this, then all the groundwork I've laid to convince them that I've gotten over the sadness in my past will be for nothing.

Tap. Tap.

When I hear a soft knock coming from the other side of the room, I take a step toward the front door. With this many Willman's running around the Brewer property this weekend, I can't just be opening the door for anyone. Lest I find myself in a three-hour conversation with my aunt who lives with her cats.

But when I look out of the peephole, there isn't anyone to be found.

Then I hear the soft tapping again and turn on a dime when I realize the knocking is coming from the adjoining door.

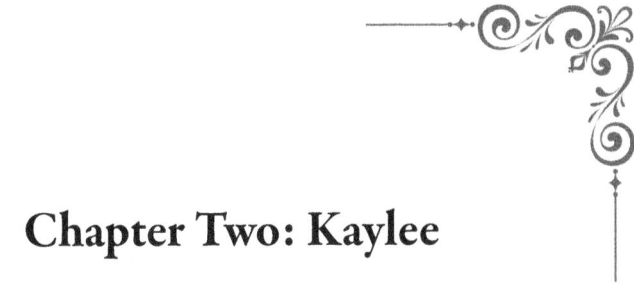

Chapter Two: Kaylee

Tap. Tap. Tap.

Standing here in my Barbie costume while Shawn's eyes roam up and down my body appraising me is awkward. Though, I can't exactly hold it against him. The blonde wig with a pink plastic mini skirt with a matching jacket and fuzzy stilettos are quite a sight to be sure. But wearing this outfit isn't the craziest thing I've done today.

Today is unlike any other I've ever had because today is the day I left my real life and hopped on a plane to pretend to be a significant part of someone else's. I tried to mentally prepare but there isn't any getting ready for a moment like this.

When the adjoining door between our hotel rooms creaks open, I swallow back my nerves. I look up at an incredibly attractive man, with dark eyes and a plastic wig. I can't help but giggle. I don't know what I was expecting from a man who paid an astronomical sum for a date to his sister's wedding, but it certainly wasn't this real-life Ken doll. Even with the costume working against him, he's breathtaking.

"Hi, I'm Kaylee." I hold out my hand and Shawn takes it in his. The feel of his skin on mine sends an unexpected tingle of heat that starts in my hand and runs all the way down my body.

"I'm Shawn. Thank you for being here. I uh, I don't make a habit of doing things like this, so the rules are fuzzy. But I'm glad you're here and I'm sorry about the costume." Shawn chuckles and puts a hand to the back of his neck flashing his massive bicep even through his suit. "My assistant is getting senile but I keep begging her not to retire."

I giggle. As Shawn and I talk and note the way his eyes never leave mine. In fact, they lock onto me with such intensity, they threaten to drown me in them. His face is perfectly symmetrical with high cheekbones, full lips, and dimples that appear when he smiles. It's impossible to look away.

"Did you have a chance to look over all the things I sent you?" Sincere worry lines crease his forehead. "My entire family is here so I need this to be believable."

"I didn't only look them over, I studied them. We met at the bakery where I work. Our first date was a walk through the farmers market."

Shawn chews on his bottom lip. "Thanks."

I don't know why he needed to hire me, but there's a sadness in his eyes that I can't ignore. All at once, I'm overwhelmed with guilt. I feel bad for him and bad for lying to him. Bad for not meeting the requirements he so clearly laid out. I may not be his ideal candidate for this job, but now that I'm here, at the very least I'll meet his expectations as a wedding date.

"Hey, I promise you, you have nothing to worry about. I will stay in character until your sister is walking down the aisle." I rest my hand on his forearm and my touch pulls a ripple of goosebumps across his skin.

Shawn pulls his arm away and straightens. "Thank you, I appreciate that. I know the contract says I won't pay you until the weekend is over, but if you want the money now for assurance, I can do that."

His mention of cash catches me off guard. "It's okay, we can stick to the contract."

It's probably for the best that we keep this weekend in perspective. This is a job after all. It isn't about lusting over the fact that Shawn could balance a cup of water on his ass or the way his quiet charm practically screams at me.

No. Taking this job is about my daughter, Rosie. The daughter I had to claim did not exist in order to be a candidate for this position in the first place. She's my very heart and soul and I would do anything in the world for her. Even when that means leaving her with my sister for a few days so I can be here, earning in one weekend what I would make in an entire year at the bakery.

I don't like leaving her, but I grew up without a mother to advocate for me. I grew up without a family at all, except for my sister Hannah. I made a promise to myself when I found out I was pregnant that my daughter would never know what it feels like to have to fend for herself in this world.

I'll do whatever it takes to give Rosie a better life than the one I had. Sometimes that means taking odd jobs in order to give her the opportunities I never had... Some are odder than others. My dream is to put her in a private school and Shawn is unknowingly going to get her there.

"Are you ready to go?" Shawn shifts his weight back and forth. "I thought it might be nice to get down there a few minutes early. If you're up for it."

"Yes, I am." I inhale through my nose and summon all my resolve. *Tonight, I am Kaylee Allen, a baker. A woman madly in love with Shawn Willman, a financier. I can do this.*

I follow Shawn out of the door of his hotel room and over to the elevator.

"Tonight we're having the rehearsal dinner at the pub on the property. They have a nice outdoor space it sounds like. It's probably all done up for Halloween too if my sister Stella has anything to say about it."

"Ah, a woman after my own heart. I love Halloween, always have, it's the best time of the year, as long as it's spooky and not scary. Who doesn't want the chance to be someone else for a night?"

"You're asking a man dressed as a life-size doll," Shawn chuckles. "Besides, I can't imagine looking like you and wanting to be anyone else even for a moment. Who could possibly be better than being you?"

His flattery makes me blush. "Plenty of people... Bella Swan for one."

"Bella who?" Shawn's eyebrows furrow together as we step out of the elevator.

"You know, Edward Cullen's one true love, the vampire... Twilight? Oh, come on, just when I thought we could be friends." I giggle.

"Oh I have a sister, I know of them, but I'm not much of a vampire enthusiast. Wait until you meet Stella, that's right up her alley. I have a feeling the two of you will be fast friends. Shall we?" Shawn holds out his elbow to me and I slip my arm through his as we make our way through the lobby.

"So tell me who I'm going to meet tonight."

"Ah, you'll see the whole crew. A lot of Willmans and some Brewers too. There's my sister Stella, the bride, and my niece McKenna. Stella can't wait to meet you, she'll talk your ear off. McKenna is six and a sweetheart. She's not big on personal space though... so, sorry in advance. Then there's the groom-to-be Spencer. He's kind of a nightmare but I'll be keeping us both far away from him if I can help it." Shawn lets out a wry chuckle.

"Okay, sounds like an interesting mix... and your parents?" I can't help but ask.

"Oh yeah, Mom and Dad will be there too, of course. Mom especially will want to know everything about you."

The way he says Mom and Dad makes a pang of jealousy stab in my stomach. Growing up in foster care, all I ever wanted were parents. I spent years fantasizing about what it would be like to have a normal home with a family who wanted to ask me about my day or get to know my new boyfriends.

Shawn leads me down the gravel path, helping steady me as I teeter on my Barbie heels across the Brew by Brewer property. This whole experience is so much better than I thought it would be. Shawn is a total gentleman and this place is incredible.

I can't help but marvel at the cheesecloth ghosts, headstones, and jack-o-lanterns hiding around every turn. Being out here is another world. I love the mix of enchanting small-town charm with the crisp mountain air.

When we arrive outside of the pub, I feel Shawn inhale. "Ready?"

"I am, are you?" I ask.

"Hell no, but here we are Barbie." Shawn chuckles and drapes his arm around me.

Shawn and I step inside the pub and a perky event planner with a warm smile and a name tag that says, *Lauren,* waves us inside. She leads us to a backroom with a vaulted ceiling and exposed beams.

The room does not disappoint. High round tables draped in white linens, soft candlelight, and gorgeous fresh floral bouquets sit everywhere the eye can see. It's hard to guess who anyone is because the room is full of gorgeous people in costume. The good genes in here are intimidating.

"Wow," I mutter under my breath. "Look at the centerpieces, they don't even look like real plants. Incredible."

"Are you okay?" Shawn asks hesitating in place.

"Yeah, I guess I've never been in a room quite like this before. It's stunning. The kind of perfect you only see in movies." My words are soft.

"Come on, it's not that good. Not even on a fancy date?" Shawn's mouth pulls to one side suspiciously.

"I've never been on a real date, at least not one where there is dancing and purple roses. I don't think I'm that kind of girl." I tuck a wild strand of blonde hair from the wig behind my ear and for a moment I worry I've gotten in over my head.

"That can't be true—" Shawn starts, but a loud, boisterous voice heading straight for us stops him in his tracks and I welcome the distraction.

"You're here! You must be Kaylee! Hi, oh my goodness, I am so excited you're here. I'm Stella, my brother has been keeping you a secret and I'm so mad at him for that." Stella is as beautiful as her big brother.

She's tall, curvy, and statuesque. She's got the same piercing dark eyes and olive skin. She's wearing the most fabulous peacock costume I've ever seen. I blush at her enthusiasm. Stella has the same charisma as her brother too and it makes me wonder what he's told her. But before I can reply, a little girl in an adorable white cat costume comes to stand beside us.

"Uncle Shawn," the girl sing-songs his name as she looks from me to Shawn and back again.

"Oh boy, here we go," Shawn laughs. "Kaylee, my sister Stella and my niece McKenna. Guys, this is Kaylee, my... girlfriend." He hesitates for a moment before he says the word girlfriend.

I hope he hasn't given too much away, but Stella's face stretches into a huge smile and she wraps her arms around me in a warm hug.

"It's nice to meet you," I say. "And congratulations! I love that you're having a Halloween wedding. It's perfect in here. What a fun idea."

"She's got good taste in weddings Shawn, I'm just saying." Stella scrunches her nose in the center. "I know we're going to be good friends. Thank you for making my brother so happy. I'm glad you're here."

His sister tells me about the wedding details. The cake. The undead bridal gown. It's all so deliciously over the top. I think she's right. We would be friends if this were real.

When Stella floats off to meet more of her guests, Shawn introduces me to his mother. As promised, she's a sweetheart of a woman. As we chat, I can't help but note that Shawn did a nice job of preparing me for this moment. He must know his mother well because he's made it exceptionally easy to answer all of the questions she throws my way.

As the room fills up with people, Shawn moves us through the room like a practiced politician. Each person I meet greets me with the same kind of enthusiasm. It isn't overwhelming, it's joyful. I can't help but wonder what it would be like to be from a family like the Willmans.

Then a familiar question prickles at me. I wonder who I would have been without all the trauma in my youth? Would I have married into a family like this? Would I have become a single mother? Would I work twelve-hour shifts at a bakery to make ends meet? Would I throw a wedding with such fanciful excess strictly because it brought me joy?

I feel a quiet resolve wash over me. I'll never know the answer to that because no one ever came along to make things right for me when I was young. Everything I have, the life that my sister and I have created together, has been earned one day at a time. That makes me smile. Then my smile grows even bigger at the thought that my daughter will never have to ask that question.

"Hey, how are you doing?" Shawn's voice paired with the warmth of his hand resting on my lower back snaps me back to the present.

"Your family is incredible. I'm having a good time." I smile up at him.

"I'm glad to hear that. Hey, I'm gonna step over and chat with Brandon for a minute." Shawn motions to a tall man with broad shoulders standing inside the door. "He's Spencer's cousin and the owner of the property. We went to school together. Will you be okay over here for a bit?"

"Yeah, of course, take your time."

"Okay, don't get into too much trouble." Shawn winks at me then leans in and plants a chaste kiss on my cheek. It sends fireworks shooting through my body and makes my knees go weak.

When he disappears, I take a moment to collect myself. Then I step toward the bar to refill my drink when I feel a tug on the hem of my plastic skirt.

I look down to see McKenna's sparkling eyes blinking up at me. "Are you Uncle Shawn's girlfriend?"

"Yes, I am." I can't help but notice how good it feels to say that, even to a child, even though it isn't true.

"You're pretty." She grins. "Like a real Barbie."

"Thank you," I laugh. With my curves and dark hair, it isn't a comparison I'm used to hearing but I'll take it.

After that, McKenna is glued to my side and I don't mind at all. She's the same age as my daughter Rosie and it's a nice reminder of why I'm putting myself through this. I'd like to live in a world where Rosie is friends with kids who grow up like McKenna in good families and with a solid education. Plus, McKenna is an absolute doll.

McKenna tells me about her school, her friends, and her stuffed animals. I learn that she likes art. I get a sample of her talent when she draws me a picture of Shawn and me on a napkin with a big heart around us. I fold it and put it into my pink bag, promising to keep it forever.

McKenna asks me about working at a bakery. Then she tells me that she'd like me to come to her house and teach her to make cookies. I don't commit to anything even though my mind is screaming, *you can come to my house and bake cookies with Rosie and me anytime.*

It's another half hour before Stella and Shawn wander toward us.

"There you are, found a friend did you?" Shawn smiles as he looks at McKenna. It melts my heart to see how much joy this little girl brings him.

"Sorry, I thought she was with my mom," Stella adds.

"Me and Kaylee are friends!" McKenna slides her little hand in mine.

"It's true," I laugh. "We're having a good time over here."

"Well thank you for watching her. But you two should go enjoy yourselves, have some drinks, dance! McKenna, let's head back to Grandma. Remember you're staying with Grandma in the morning while I get ready for the wedding. It's good for you to practice not running off." Stella takes her daughter by the hand and I see a familiar pang of tension in her face as McKenna wiggles away and heads for the dance floor. Stella needs more support, any mom could recognize the look.

"Kids," Shawn says, the sadness behind his eyes suddenly reappearing.

"Yeah, tell me about it. It isn't totally McKenna's fault. Mom's getting a little old to watch her to be honest. I think it's tough on both of them. I worry Mom can't keep up and I think she does too even though she won't admit it," Stella says.

"I could watch McKenna in the morning so you can get ready. I mean, *we* could, Shawn and me, if you don't mind. That way you can get ready in peace and you won't have to worry about her running off. Maybe your mom could even join you." I look at Shawn and he raises his eyebrows in surprise.

"Are you sure?" Stella looks from me to her brother.

"Of course," Shawn says. "I wouldn't have thought to offer, but I'd never turn downtime with my Kenna girl."

"Thank you. I will take you up on it, I appreciate you two," Stella says.

As Stella walks away, Shawn turns to me and lowers his voice. "That was nice of you to offer to help my sister. You don't have to babysit, you can enjoy your morning. I know it isn't a part of our agreement."

"I wouldn't have offered if I didn't mean it. Your sister is amazing and I'm happy to help."

"That's sweet of you, thank you." Shawn traces his hand down my arm and I try not to melt with his touch. "Stella is something. I've always felt so protective of her. It makes me furious that she's marrying such a jackass. Do you have any siblings?"

"Yes, actually, one sister, Hannah. I'm the oldest, so I understand. I've taken care of Hannah all my life and sometimes the guys she dates are total train wrecks. Thankfully she hasn't married any of them, at least not yet." I roll my eyes at the memory of Hannah's last boyfriend. "But spending the morning with McKenna will be great. We'll find something fun to do with her."

"Yeah, it will be great. I'll have the two best-looking ladies on my arm, how lucky am I? For now, why don't you let me buy you a drink?"

Shawn and I laugh the night away. I admit, I let myself get carried away in the lie Shawn and I are creating. I lean into his touch. I laugh at his jokes. I look up at him like he's my favorite person. I convince myself that he actually might be.

I hear one hundred stories from one hundred people about Shawn. It's fun to pretend. Only, Shawn seems to be exactly who he says he is, confident, charming, and sweet. But if those things are true, why is there a hint of sadness behind his eyes? Why did he need to hire me instead of coming with a real date? Surely anyone would be proud to be here on his arm.

With as much fun as I'm having with him, I know I need to stay focused. I can't fall for a man who doesn't know anything about me. At the end of the day, people like me don't end up in families like this. I'm here for my daughter and I can't lose sight of that.

LATER THAT NIGHT WHEN I'm back in the privacy of my own hotel room, I call my sister Hannah. She confirms that Rosie is having the time of her life, eating pancakes for every meal and watching movies in her pajamas until the afternoon. It makes me ache to see my girl, I'm not used to being away from her like this.

Before we hang up, I give Hannah a summary of my interactions with Shawn thus far and she immediately dubs him, Mr. Perfectly Plastic. It seems fitting given not only our costumes but the way he carries himself. Shawn is a perfect gentleman through and through.

I only hope I can keep my head out of the dream house while I get through this weekend.

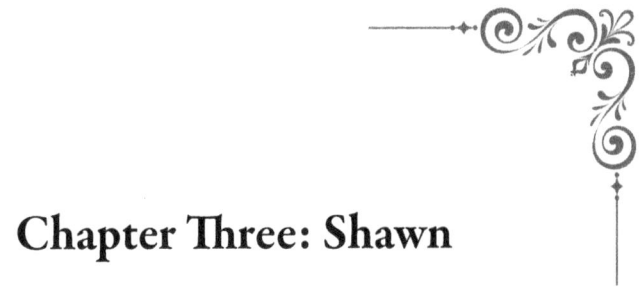

Chapter Three: Shawn

The next day, I wake up with the sun and talk to Brandon Brewer about securing a golf cart for what I hope will be the perfect date with two perfect ladies. Once I have the keys in my hands, I spend the morning whipping McKenna and Kaylee around the property.

Kaylee looks beautiful dressed down in a sweatshirt and tight-fitting jeans. Her hair is tossed into a messy bun and there isn't an ounce of makeup on her face. I could get used to seeing more of her like this, being around her brings out something in me that has been dormant for a long time.

The three of us explore every inch of the seventy-four-acre property. Whirling by the cat cafe, the pub, the pumpkin patch, and out past the greenhouses. McKenna squeals with delight and clings to Kaylee as I bump our cart through the woods behind the Brewer hotel. When we arrive at a clearing, I park the golf cart.

"Everyone out! We've officially arrived at our date, part two." I make my announcement with the kind of dramatic excitement only a six-year-old can appreciate. But Kaylee humors me, smiling alongside McKenna.

"Uncle Shawn, what are we doing?" McKenna asks.

"Oh, I don't know... anyone up for breakfast in the woods?" I pull the brown basket out of the back of the golf cart and hold it up.

"You packed snacks? I'm so impressed," Kaylee says.

"I aim to please." I wink at her and it pulls a beautiful smile across her pink lips. I spread out the blanket over the top of the crunchy leaves that have fallen from the trees in the forest.

Kaylee opens the basket and peers inside, then her forehead wrinkles, and she scrunches her nose in the center. "It's all sweets."

"That's right because Uncle Shawn is the coolest." I laugh and McKenna cheers. "Don't worry, there's another bag back there with healthy food too, I wasn't sure what you liked."

"All dessert all the time is actually my favorite. You should see some of the things we come up with at the bakery..." As Kaylee tells me about her job, her face lights up and she's that much more stunning.

"Can I tell you something, I wish I could go to the bakery and try some of your creations. I want to see the town you live in, meet your sister. Stop by for a bit and see that part of your life. This thing between us is one-sided. You've met everyone in my family and you fit in perfectly, but I don't know anything about you." I worry I've gone too far, but before Kaylee can respond, McKenna holds her hand up.

"Uh, hello, her name is Kaylee and she's your girlfriend and she knows how to make so many cookies." McKenna puts her hand on her hip and looks from Kaylee to me and back again.

"That's right, thank you for clearing that up," I laugh.

"What do you want to know?" Kaylee asks.

"Everything," I tell her honestly.

When she gives me the green light, I ask as many questions as I can. Kaylee answers them, though she doesn't offer much beyond the facts. I can't tell if she's holding back because McKenna's here or if she wants to keep me at arm's length. If she does, I can't blame her. We didn't exactly meet under normal circumstances.

"This is my best day ever," McKenna shouts as she holds up a flower she's plucked from the ground.

"Me too," I add. I reach across the blanket and give Kaylee's arm a gentle squeeze. I admit to myself that this isn't for show, McKenna hardly cares what we're doing. It's because I want to be closer to Kaylee. In fact, I feel like I can't possibly get close enough.

I'm overwhelmed by how nice it is to have Kaylee here with me. Is this what family life could be like? It certainly isn't the experience I had with my ex. With Kaylee, I have the feeling what you see is what you get and I like that. She's caring and sweet. There's a depth to her that I didn't expect.

"Can I go pick flowers?" McKenna stands, rocking up on her tiptoes and I don't know how anyone is ever going to say no to this kid for anything.

"Yes," I say.

"Stay where we can see you," Kaylee adds. The way she takes care of McKenna is so natural. "She's a good kid."

"She is, I worry about my sister though. She does it all on her own, Spencer sits back and lets her run herself into the ground and now she's marrying him."

Kaylee scoffs and rolls her eyes. "Typical."

"What does that mean? You're cynical about love too, I didn't take you for the type," I chuckle.

"No, I'm not cynical about love at all. I think that there are a lot of lazy dads out there who look like good parents because moms like your sister are working overtime. It's frustrating. But I know they aren't all like that. I know that love, real love, isn't like that. I want love in my life, only I'm choosy about it. I want the forever kind of love, nothing less. I want someone who comes into my world and stays there in the good parts and the messy parts too." Kaylee's voice is soft but confident.

"I just might want to run away from my world and into yours," I tell her before I can stop myself.

"I might let you." Kaylee looks at me, her dark eyes glittering in the sun.

I reach across the blanket and take her hand in mine. Then I lean in toward her. My heart is beating fast in my chest. All I can think is, I'm so lucky. I'm lucky in love for the first time in my life. Lucky that she is the person who responded to my advertisement. Lucky to be here with her.

I put a hand on her cheek and sweep away a loose strand of silky hair that blows in front of her face. "I—"

Ouch! Ouch!

The sound of McKenna shrieking then crying has me springing to my feet. My heart pounds in my chest and my head turns on a swivel to look for her.

"She's okay Shawn, she's right there past the tree. It looks like she just tripped." Kaylee gets to her feet but I can't take her word for it.

I've made the mistake of not trusting my instincts before and I won't do it again. I sprint to the treeline, my heart pounding in my chest. "Kenna!" I shout.

When I reach her, McKenna looks up at me with tears in her eyes and her words come out between sobs. "I fell off the rock."

"Are you okay? What hurts?" I demand. "Why were you climbing on that rock to begin with?"

"Uncle Shawn, don't yell at me," McKenna wails.

"I'm not, I'm just... I need to make sure you're okay." My breath catches in my throat.

I don't even notice Kaylee beside me until I feel her cool hand on my back. "Hey, Shawn honey, she's fine. She's okay." She pats my back gently.

"Yeah," I agree, trying to get a hold of myself. I scoop up McKenna and walk her back to the blanket. Then I sit her down and gulp for air.

Panic burns my throat and I look at the little girl that holds so much of my heart. My son, if he were still here, would be the same age as McKenna is right now. But he's gone because I didn't want to start a fight with my ex. Because I chose the path of least resistance and now my barometer for what is and is not an emergency is totally fucked anytime I'm around someone I love.

McKenna nuzzles into Kaylee's chest and then resumes her flower picking. When McKenna is out of earshot, Kaylee looks up at me. "Are you okay?"

"Yes, I'm a little overprotective I guess." My words are clipped and I don't mean them to be, but I don't like this part of myself. I couldn't be a father. I should at least figure out how to be an uncle.

"Okay," Kaylee hesitates, waiting for me to elaborate but I don't. So she continues, "I think I'll go help her find some flowers for a bit."

As Kaylee wanders away, all I can think is that McKenna's fall is exactly what I needed to bring me back down to reality. Who am I kidding? Kaylee is here, playing a role because that's what I'm paying her to do. I will not fall in love with Kaylee, not now, not ever because I can't keep the people I love safe. I can't go through loving and losing again because I might never recover.

An hour later, I'm trying to get out of my own head when I get a text from my sister telling me that it's McKenna's turn to get her hair done. As we are loading the golf cart an older couple walks by and gives us a wave.

"Hello, what a cute family." The woman calls out to us.

McKenna gives her an enthusiastic wave.

"Thank you," Kaylee says, a sweet smile resting on her lips.

"We're not a family," I call to the woman. "I don't have any kids and I don't want any."

"Oh... uh, okay. Well... enjoy the fresh air." The woman looks flustered and she turns away from me.

As we climb into the golf cart, Kaylee locks eyes with me. She's not blinking and her brows are furrowed in the center.

"What?" I ask.

"That was a pretty aggressive response to, *cute kid,* don't you think?" She lets out a humorless chuckle. "I had no idea you were so anti-kid. It's too bad. You'd be one of the good dads and the world needs more of those." There isn't any bite to Kaylee's words, but she has no idea what she's talking about.

"No, I wouldn't."

McKenna climbs out of the golf cart in search of the flower bouquet she left behind.

I turn back to Kaylee. "What do you want, an army of kids?"

Kaylee straightens in her seat. "Shawn, I'm willing to do this little pretend thing with you this weekend, but I won't lie to you about that. I do want kids. They're the best and I should be so lucky to have them. I grew up in foster care without a family, so having one, or the ability to create one means something different to me."

That's more evidence that Kaylee and I together would never work outside of this bubble I've created. It's too bad, she's a sweetheart and she's made me happier than I've been in a long time but we're heading two very different places.

"Understood. Sorry, I didn't mean to offend you." Then I add, "For the record, you'd be a great mom and I hope you get that someday."

"Thank you for saying that and it's okay. But it is time to get McKenna back. We should go anyway, we have a long night ahead of us." Kaylee calls McKenna over and wraps an arm around her as she climbs into the golf cart.

"Right."

As I pull the cart out of the clearing, I feel a pang of sadness well in me. I think I let myself buy into the story I created about Kaylee. That she could somehow be the right person for me. That I was finally lucky in love.

Chapter Four: Kaylee

After our date with McKenna, I step into my own hotel room and close the door behind me to get ready for Stella's big day. Despite the awkwardness of the latter part of the morning, I can hardly wait to spend more time with Shawn. I hope that we can talk things over, and I hope to get more clarity on why he is so against the idea of children.

The costume in bag number two doesn't disappoint. It's got to be the sexiest zombie dress I've ever seen. It's a black, sequin, ribbed corset with a short skirt made of tulle and lace. I make a note to thank Shawn's assistant for making me look great and finding costumes that accentuate my favorite parts of my body, on the off chance I ever get to meet her.

I get ready without a moment to spare and as I'm spraying my hair into place, I hear three taps on the door. When I open it, Shawn is staring at me with his signature, brilliant smile holding a container of costume makeup. "Can you help me with this?"

"I can do that," I tell him.

Shawn sits on the chair by my bed and I get to work on making him look like a zombie. "Thank you and I'm sorry things got intense earlier. What do you say we make tonight the best night ever?"

"I'm sorry too. Making tonight the best night ever sounds good to me."

THE WEDDING ITSELF flies by in a flash. The ceremony starts and finishes in only ten minutes and even then, it isn't without its problems. The candle on the altar refuses to stay lit. The floral arch starts shedding petals in the middle of the ceremony. McKenna refuses to walk down the aisle with her basket of flowers.

Spencer seems too intoxicated to speak clearly. But the most shocking part of the ceremony is Stella herself. Though she looks immaculate in her black, Victorian gown, something seems off.

There's a vacancy in her eyes and when it's her turn to say her vows, she simply promises to keep on making sacrifices for the sake of her daughter. It's a sentiment I can understand and for the first time, I wonder what Stella may have had to give up in the name of being a mother.

When the officiant pronounces the couple husband and wife, Spencer seems to spring back to life. He gropes at Stella's breast and high-fives one of the groomsmen.

Shawn, who has thus far been tense and stoic, leans over to me and whispers. "What a shit show."

I don't reply. Though, I'll give him that the ceremony isn't exactly romantic. In fact, I find myself thinking that the wedding planner deserves an award for taking it all in stride and keeping the perfectly poised smile plastered on her face.

By the time an hour has passed and we're sitting at our table in the banquet room at the reception, things feel a little less tense. Shawn looks as handsome as ever in his zombie costume. Which in reality is only a bit of costume makeup paired with a suit that fits like a glove and is torn in all the right places. I feel sexy in my matching black, undead dress with high boots.

Stella is making her way around the room chatting with the guests. McKenna has taken over the dance floor with a few other children, and Spencer has all but disappeared into a bottle of whiskey.

I've gotten used to the warm comfort of being tucked into Shawn's side. I like the feeling of being his other half more than I want to admit to myself. In short, he's everything I never knew could exist in a man. He's easy to love. I feel guilty about how badly I don't want my time with him to end.

Lauren, the wedding planner, stands at the front of the room. She uses a fork to tap the side of a champagne flute until the room falls silent. "Hi there, just a warning that if you don't have anything in your glass, now is the time to fill up as I invite the brother of the bride to come to give the toast."

Shawn shifts in his chair and rubs his palms on the top of his thighs. "Here we go, time for my speech in honor of the happy couple. I don't know if I can do this in good faith."

"You can. Not for Spencer, but for your sister. You'll be amazing." I give the top of his thigh a gentle squeeze and it makes his dimples appear.

Shawn takes my hand in his and plants a sweet kiss on the back of it. "I'll be right back."

I watch Shawn make his way to the front of the room. All eyes are on him and it feels right. That's exactly where they should be. He's at home in front of this crowd, their prized possession. Deserving of all the accolades he receives. Best of brothers. Best of sons. Best of uncles. And for tonight, best of boyfriends.

Shawn clears his throat as he takes the microphone. "On behalf of my sister, I'd like to thank you all for coming here tonight to celebrate. You know, when Kaylee told me that I was going to be an uncle, I couldn't help but wonder how it happened."

Laughter bubbles through the crowd.

"Oh, I mean, not literally you guys, gross." He chuckles. "It was unfathomable to me that my baby sister was old enough to kiss boys, especially boys like Spencer... but here we are."

More pockets of laughter ripple and my eyes dart to Stella. She's looking adoringly at her big brother. Spencer on the other hand is only looking at his phone.

"My sister was my favorite person until my niece came along that is. Stella is one hell of a mom, McKenna, I wouldn't mess with her sweetheart. But if you need anything, Uncle Shawn has got you covered. Seriously, Stella and McKenna are angels on earth and they deserve the world. Spencer, I've never understood you man, but one thing I know for sure is that you've got a good one there. You have a big opportunity to have the kind of life that most men dream of...Don't mess it up."

Shawn continues his toast, gushing over his niece and being fiercely protective of his sister. Listening to him talk makes my heart swell. I can't help but wonder why he's so vehemently opposed to the idea of children when he's obviously a natural with them.

I watch him more closely, searching for traces of sadness, and it's still there. His every word is thoughtful or is it controlled? Every gesture is graceful or is it tense? He leans on his natural charisma to carry him through the toast but I can see the tension in his jaw. I notice the way he swallows hard when Spencer's name leaves his mouth... and there's something else too, though I can't put my finger on exactly what it is.

One thing is for certain, McKenna is a lucky little girl. Whether or not her father turns out to be the man Stella hopes he is, McKenna will always have her Uncle Shawn. It's a beautiful sentiment that brings a tear to my eyes.

Shawn concludes his toast by begrudgingly welcoming Spencer to the family and raising his glass in honor of the couple. Pride swells in me, that couldn't have been easy for him but he was perfect. I welcome Shawn back to the table with a hug.

As the reception winds on, Shawn says goodnight to his parents. As the crowd dwindles, I get more and more comfortable being the woman on Shawn's arm. He introduces me to every person in the room and he doesn't use many of the details from the emails we exchanged. Instead, he tells the truth. Or rather the parts of the truth he knows.

This is Kaylee, she loves to bake. This is Kaylee, she's amazing with children. This is Kaylee, she loves vampires, plants, and music. This is Kaylee, she makes me smile like no one else.

With each compliment, I feel a familiar refrain echo in my mind. *I wish this was my real life.* By the time Shawn leads me out onto the dance floor, I'm seeing stars. He whirls me around the room and I give into him completely. He leads and for once, I'm happy to follow.

When the song turns slow, I look up at Shawn. He pulls me in close and brushes a strand of hair away from my face. He wraps his arms around me. His eyes dip to my cleavage and linger for a minute too long.

"Are you having a good time? I mean, for what it is?" His voice is barely audible and the sensation of his lips brushing against my ear is intoxicating.

"I am having the best time with you." I look up at him from underneath my lashes.

His stare threatens to break me. I want to give myself to this man, heart, body, and mind. Shawn buries one hand in the back of my hair and his mouth inches closer to mine. The heat from his breath dances across my lips and it makes my heart pound in my chest.

Shawn leans in closer and though our lips aren't actually touching yet, I can already feel the electrical current crackling between us. Maybe everyone around us is watching or maybe they aren't here anymore at all. I have no idea because Shawn is all I can see.

When our lips finally touch, all the air is sucked out of the room. My heart pounds wild and off-rhythm in my chest. My fantasy world bubbles to life. Warmth blooms low in my stomach. I kiss him back. I put my hand on the back of his neck. I part his lips with my tongue.

He kisses me with a hunger I didn't expect. It's frantic, desperate, and... real.

From there, things escalate quickly. His hands are on my hips guiding me off the dancefloor. His mouth is on my ear. Each touch thrills me. Each whisper feels like a promise.

After that, it's a blur. We're tucked away in the back corner of the room. Tucked behind a black backdrop and lost in our own world. Shawn's face is buried in my cleavage and my thigh is around his waist. He pins me against the wall.

His hand makes its way up my thigh and I can't imagine being anywhere else with anyone else right now. Shawn kisses me like I'm his. Like he owns me. Like tonight is all we have, and it might be, so I'm going to make it count.

I'm panting, barely holding on to the last shred of reality that Shawn is kissing away when suddenly, the music stops. A loud booming sound comes crackling through the speaker right beside us and it makes me jump.

"Uh, hello? Anyone want to acknowledge the fact that this is my party?" Spencer's mouth is too close to the microphone and the sheer volume of it brings the chatter in the ballroom to a halt.

I pull my dress down and smooth the front of it. Shawn laughs as he tries to hide the massive bulge in his pants. He takes me by the hand and we step out from behind the backdrop, Shawn's attention is focused on Spencer.

"What are you about to do, dude?" Shawn mutters his question under his breath.

The microphone pops and crackles as Spencer breathes into it. "You all know I knocked up Stella and now she's stuck with me. So there's that." Spencer slurs his words and laughs in a crass chuckle that rubs me the wrong way. "But there's something I need all my friends to know."

Shawn goes on high alert, straightening his posture, and taking a step toward the front of the room.

Spencer continues. "Stella is beautiful, but she used to be a lot hotter like the rest of the bridal party, am I right gentlemen? Whoop! Well, it was just baby weight and I know she'll get her body back someday. I'm cutting her calories."

My eyes widen and my jaw falls open in absolute horror. Shawn pulls his hand away from me and is flying toward the front of the room.

Spencer laughs, "I don't know about the stretch marks though. Yuk—"

But that's all he gets out. In an instant, Shawn is beside him mumbling something that doesn't sound friendly and his hand is wrapped around Spencer's wrist. It seems the men in Spencer's family are on the same page as Shawn. The Brewer men practically form a wall as they head toward the front of the room.

Spencer jerks the microphone away from Shawn and puts it back to his mouth. "Chill, chill, it's fine. Stella, you're fine aren't you?"

I glance at Stella over the top of my glass and she looks anything but fine, as she should.

"We're done here." Shawn puts a heavy hand on Spencer's shoulder and Spencer turns, fist balled.

I hold my breath along with everyone else in the room to see what's going to happen next. The two of them squaring off is a joke. Shawn could annihilate him in a single punch even if Spencer were sober, which he clearly is not.

As Shawn lifts Spencer off his feet in an attempt to drag him off the dancefloor, Spencer grabs the microphone one last time.

This time Spencer's words aren't a shout, they're steady, controlled. He enunciates every last one of them. "I am so sick of you Shawn. McKenna isn't your kid. Stella isn't your responsibility. How does it feel knowing that I have everything you wanted? A wife that won't leave me. A kid that's still alive. Doesn't taste good, does it? Everyone in here knows the only reason you hate me is that you're jealous that your kid died and mine didn't. But here's the thing, you did that. You let him die. So next time you want to hate someone, look in the mirror."

Chapter Five: Shawn

I blackout for a moment, blind rage taking over. I can't say exactly what happens next, but I know I get at least one solid punch in before I'm being lifted off of Spencer. I look behind me to see Brandon Brewer and his brothers carrying me backward and I don't fight them. In fact, I'm glad they're here.

I don't know if I could have stopped myself. Spencer crossed a line that he can't come back from. I'm afraid I wouldn't have stopped pounding my niece's father into the ground until he didn't get up and maybe not even then.

When I open my eyes, every muscle I have is still clenched and my blood boils in my stomach. My body trembles with fury. Brandon hands me a bottle of water and I nod, assuring him that I won't go after Spencer again, though I don't know whether or not I'm telling the truth.

There's a calm that falls over the room after the storm of chaos dwindles and that's when I see Spencer being escorted out of his own wedding by two of Brandon's brothers. As they exit with him, things start to get quiet and the room spins.

I close my eyes and see my son. I hear my ex-wife's voice on the phone telling me that her new boyfriend would be taking my son to a baseball game. I said I didn't feel good about it. I didn't know the guy. I didn't trust him. But she insisted.

My ex lied to me so often that when she told me it was happening with or without my consent, I actually thought to myself, *at least she's telling me the truth, that's a win. That's a win.* Nausea rises in my throat.

She threatened to keep him from me the way she did every time we disagreed about anything large or small. So, I didn't say no. I didn't get in my truck and drive out to her house and pull my son out of that car the way I should have. I didn't keep him safe. One drunk driving accident later, my son paid the ultimate price.

My memories settle over my head, threatening to drown me. I'm stuck back in time and I can't come up for air no matter what I do. My chest caves in on itself as I gulp for breath. I feel like I might fall over and someone slides a chair in my direction. I flop onto it and put my head between my knees. I can't say how long I stay like this because when you live in the past, time is always stopped.

"Shawn. Shawn. Are you okay?"

I hear my name and it punctures my thoughts, but I don't recognize the voice until a cool hand lands softly on my chest. I look up at Kaylee as sweat trickles down my face.

"Let's go outside for a minute, get some fresh air okay? You don't look good." Her voice is kind and her hand on my skin helps regulate my breath.

"I look fine. There isn't a scratch on me." I sit up in my seat. "This is a zombie costume, it's makeup, remember?" I attempt a joke but it falls flat.

"No, your skin is pale and you're sweating. Let's step outside." Kaylee takes my hand in hers and pulls me gently. I get to my feet and follow behind her still in a daze.

We make it out into the courtyard. The crisp, autumn night air hits me and brings with it the realization that Kaylee now knows about my son. She must have so many questions. She's probably even upset with me and maybe she should be. It's a big thing to omit from the story of my life.

Kaylee sits on the ledge of the fountain and tugs on my arm, pulling me down beside her. "Are you okay?" Kaylee asks, a gentle hand resting on my thigh.

"I am. I can't believe what an asshole my sister married. I haven't lost control like that in a long while but he was—" My adrenaline picks back up just thinking about it.

"Rightfully so." Kaylee gives my thigh a gentle squeeze and stops me from spiraling back into a rage. "What you did to him is exactly what he deserved. He was grossly out of line."

I clear my throat. "You must be mad that I wasn't honest with you about my son."

"I'm not. You don't owe me anything. But I am sorry you had to experience the unimaginable. You're an even stronger man than I thought you were." She looks up at me and something about her calm, caring, demeanor disarms me.

A topic that I've gone out of my way to avoid for years bubbles up on the surface. Before I know it, everything comes spilling out. I give Kaylee the details of my short-lived marriage and the toxic situation with my ex-wife. I tell her about the lies and the arguments.

Then, I tell Kaylee about my son. Not about the kid that died, but the one that lived every day to the fullest. The six-year-old with the toothless smile who loved baseball. The one who said I was his favorite person. The one who wanted to be like me when he grew up, but never got the chance.

Kaylee listens intently as I admit to the sleepless nights and bad dreams that have plagued me ever since he left. I tell her about the first twenty seconds of every morning when I wake up and forget that he isn't here anymore.

As I talk, there isn't any judgment in Kaylee's eyes. She doesn't ask me to explain or give me questions to answer. Instead, she lets me say whatever comes out. She holds my hand. She cries with me. The way she listens is a gift I didn't know I needed.

Shedding all those layers of guilt, sadness, and joy that have been repressed for so long makes me feel like more of a man. I'm like the autumn trees letting go of old leaves and making room for something new.

A cool breeze whips through the air and I take off my torn zombie-suit-jacket and drape it over her shoulders. Then I put my arm around her and slide her body into my side, letting my eyes dip down into the cleavage poking out of the top of her dress.

"So that's it. That's the reason I had to hire you. I needed to show all of these people that I'm going to be alright because I am. My life doesn't look the way I thought it would, but I'm okay. And having you here is more than okay, it's pretty wonderful. You were always going to be the person who answered my ad. It was always going to be you and me here, like this. I believe that." My words are barely above a whisper.

When Kaylee turns to look away and I catch her chin then turn her face up to mine. Her eyes sparkle the reflection of the moon back at me and I'm overwhelmed with gratitude to be sitting here with the most beautiful woman I've ever met.

She inches her face closer to mine until our mouths are nearly touching. I can feel a zap of electricity bouncing back and forth between us. I close my eyes and plant my lips on hers, I'm immediately lost in the same fire I felt earlier. Every single fiber of my being responds. It's fireworks, it's electricity, it's coming home.

For a beautiful, perfect moment, Kaylee lets me hold her there. Kissing me back with the same intensity. But then, she hesitates and pulls back the slightest bit.

"What's wrong?" I brush a strand of hair away from her face.

"There's something I should tell you..." She taps her foot and rolls her fingers into the tulle fabric on the end of her zombie costume.

I can tell she's nervous, but I have no idea why. Anything she has to say won't negate all that's building between us.

"What is it?" I take her hands in mine. "You can tell me anything."

Boom.

Before Kaylee can say another word, the door to the courtyard swings open with a crash, and Spencer steps out. In an instant, I'm on my feet.

"Hey, it's my party and I'm back. Sorry about that bro I got carried away." Spencer's voice is like nails on a chalkboard. He's loud. He's rude. He's drunk and he's got an impressive shiner on his eye.

Kaylee gets to her feet too and when Spencer approaches us, she puts a hand on his chest and talks to him through clenched teeth. "I think your wife is looking for you." Her words come out with a snap.

Spencer chuckles then holds up his hands defensively before heading back toward the entrance.

When he hesitates at the door and turns back to us I shout before I can stop myself. "Not a fucking word from you."

Kaylee turns to me, her pretty mouth twisted up into a sexy smirk. "Forget him. Hey, I have an idea, why don't we go see some of those hidden rooms around the property. It sounds like fun doesn't it? I mean, things are pretty much wrapped up in there for the night." Kaylee leans into me and I don't protest. I know as well as anyone that if I step through those doors right now it's only going to be trouble. "Come on, let's go play for a little bit."

"I like the sound of that."

Chapter Six: Kaylee

A half-hour later, we're wandering the back rooms, the hotel is great. There's an air of mystery that probably isn't much of a stretch for a building that is over a hundred years old. But on top of its natural spooky factors, the whole thing is all dolled up for Halloween.

As we walk hand in hand, there are witches, werewolves, and zombies around every turn. Black plastic bats with red glowing eyes hang unsuspectingly in corners. The halls are illuminated by black lights and there's eerie music being piped in through the speakers.

The experience touches all of my senses and transports me into another world. It seems to do the same for Shawn because his face is no longer pinched into tight lines. Instead, an easy smile turns up the corners of his mouth and he rubs his thumbs across the back of my hands.

As we wander an abandoned back corridor turning doorknobs, I gaze into a mirror only to have a ghost appear on the other side. It sends me leaping into the air with a laugh.

"Don't worry, I'll protect you sweetheart." Shawn chuckles as he wraps his arm around me and pulls me close.

When we try the last door handle before the stairwell, the lock clicks open. My jaw falls open in surprise and I look at Shawn. "We found one of the hidden rooms! I can't believe it. I was starting to think they were urban legends."

I push open the door and peer inside the room. It's only dimly lit by a single glowing orange bulb in a lamp on a bedside table. There's an old bookshelf and a dusty, stained glass window. On the wall is a large painting of an old woman with ominous eyes in a gold frame. In the center of the room is a magnificent cherry oak, four-poster-bed complete with black mosquito net curtains.

I fumble to find the lights, but when I flip the switch, they don't come on. Instead, the switch seems to start up an old scratchy-sounding record player sitting in the corner of the room. It lets out some sort of tinny romance song.

"Wow," Shawn says, and I follow his line of sight.

When my eyes make it up to the ceiling, I see a massive mirror hanging above the bed. "Maybe we should put that to good use." I put my hand low on Shawn's back.

"Yeah, I can think of a few things I'd like to see from every angle." His eyes roam up and down my body and it makes me flush with heat.

I look up at the mirror imagining Shawn's naked body in the reflection, but this time it lights up with another ghostly face. It makes me jump and I squeal with laughter. "Got me again!"

Shawn lets out a deep belly laugh then closes the door to the old bedroom behind us. "You've got to be the most squeamish zombie I've ever met. But you make up for it by being the most beautiful too."

From there, we're ignited. The tension building between us boils over. Shawn's hand presses against my cheek. Then his lips slide against my mouth. Shawn curls a hand around my neck, his fingers run over my fake jewelry, and he parts my lips with his tongue. As he pulls back, his teeth latch onto my lower lip, gently pulling it with him.

He settles his hand gently on my shoulder and it all feels so natural. I start to think that maybe this thing between us could work. After what I heard in the courtyard it's obvious that Shawn doesn't hate kids. He's just hurt. Watching him talk about losing his son was painful. But it also revealed a depth of character I had no idea was lurking below the surface.

He moves us toward the bed and I go willingly. But in the back of my mind, there's a faint voice telling me I should stop this right now, or at least pause it. I need to come clean and tell him about Rosie then let him decide whether he can handle who I really am. But I don't want to make him relive his pain. Besides, right now it's hard to think about anything other than the way his mouth feels on mine and the way his hands dig into the back of my hair.

Shawn wraps his arms around me, burying his face into the nape of my neck. His voice is almost a growl. "I didn't expect you, but I want you, all of you."

When he throws me onto my back on the bed, the hotel sheets smell clean, despite the fact that the room is probably meant to look abandoned. A small part of me hopes that the face in the mirror doesn't double as a camera, but the thought is quickly pushed away by the fact that Shawn is climbing on top of me and caging me in with his arms.

The torn parts of the shirt he's wearing fall over us like a blanket and I laugh. But the sound is quickly stripped away and turned into a breathless moan when he starts working on my neck.

Shawn leaves messy, open-mouthed kisses all over me. My neck, my face, his tongue licking its way back into my mouth. I run my hands over his shoulders, and brush them along his gel-crusted hair.

His hand settles on my side and then up higher, curling against my breast and fondling it through the sequin top of my zombie dress. My breathing picks up and I can feel his erection press against my inner thigh through his pants.

He leans back to slide my dress down over my hips and there's cold air against me where his body had been pressed a moment before. Between the two of us, we're able to reduce my dress to nothing more than a pile of fabric on the floor in seconds. His clothes are quick to follow.

Then Shawn's curling over me and we're kissing again, his thigh slots between my own spread legs. I'm already slick in my panties and the pressure of his leg against my folds makes that wetness dribble out even more.

"Look at you. Look at your curves, look at this body." Shawn's voice is breathy as he grinds his leg into me. "You're fucking perfect."

My hips jerk of their own accord. I rock back into him, rubbing myself against his thigh. I reach out, and fumble with his ass, pulling him closer until I can feel him rolling down against me, teasing my opening with his firm length.

His hands go back to my mounds and he fondles them. Shawn's thumb rubs over my pert nipple and then pinches it. I whine and buck harder against his thigh. Pressure builds up inside of me, twisting, winding me higher and higher.

Shawn pulls away enough to slide a hand between my legs. He runs his fingers along my slit, grinding the pre-cum wet cotton against my nub. There's no actual skin-on-skin contact. It's only the prickling grind of wet fabric over my skin and the heat of him breathing into the side of my neck, dragging his tongue up over the line of my jaw.

I look up into the mirror and I like what I see. Shawn's naked body is firmly on top of mine. The muscles of his backside taut, flexed, bulging. I see my own reflection change when he slips the layer of thin fabric out of the way and works me open. Shawn grinds his palm against my clit then plunges two fingers inside.

I'm supposed to be out here keeping things professional, earning money for my daughter's education, not falling into bed with an almost stranger, and certainly not falling in love with him. Yet there's not a single part of me that wants this to stop.

I've never wanted anyone more. All I can hear is the faint creaking of the bed, my own moans, and Shawn's still heaving breath. The fabric of my panties is absolutely soaked when he rips them off me. Even in the dark of the dimly lit room, I can make out the way that Shawn brings his fingers up to his mouth and licks them clean.

He kisses down my body and traces the outline of my puffy lips with his tongue. I do my best to throw my legs even further open. After that, I lose myself in him. I give in as he sucks, licks, and tastes me. He stays there until I'm bucking against him and screaming his name into a pillow.

It's a frenzy of hands roaming and hearts beating. It's white-hot desire. He holds me there as I ride the wave of orgasm that rocks through me. The heat crashes through my veins in a heavy, drowning sort of flow and Shawn is all I can see. Sweet, sexy Shawn. The best Halloween treat I've ever had.

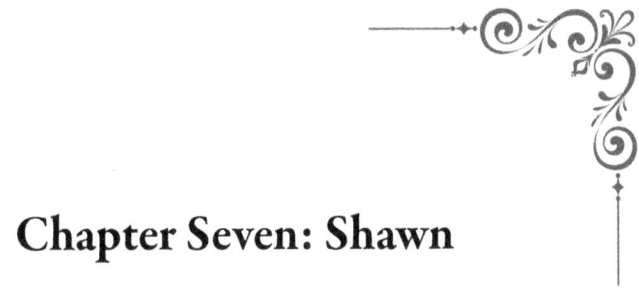

Chapter Seven: Shawn

Kaylee's body is wracked with tremors, but letting her recover is the last thing on my mind. My member throbs, my tip glistens and my body burns with desire for her as I draw my face away from her thighs.

I pause for a moment and take her in, committing every last detail to memory. My fingertips trace the outline of her beautiful body with a feather-light touch. My eyes run across every inch of her supple skin. I don't know if I can convince her to stay in my world beyond this weekend and just in case she leaves, this is how I want to remember her.

When I can't take it any longer, I move over the top of her. My body anchors hers to the top of the quilt. Her soft, rounded edges pressed into my hard lines are an intoxicating combination.

Kaylee nips at my earlobe and runs her tongue along the length of my neck, the sensation is electrifying. I wrap my hand around the back of her neck and bury my fingers in her hair. I bring my mouth to hers and claim her lips, sucking, licking, and parting them with my tongue. But our kiss doesn't last long because I'm more than ready to bury myself inside of her.

I align myself with her slit and I'm already pulsating when I plunge deep inside of Kaylee in a single, mighty, thrust. She gasps at my size, but she takes in every inch of me. I feel her walls stretch around me, accommodating my girth.

Once I'm in, I rock in and out of her slowly, savoring the moment. I feel her clench and grip along the entire length of my shaft. Kaylee arches her back and moves in time with me until it's hard to tell where she ends and I begin.

Tingles whip across my body and my breathing comes faster until I lose control and hammer her into the mattress. Soft moans escape her pretty mouth in time with my thrusts. Her velvet, soft, folds quiver and Kaylee calls out my name through clenched teeth.

She wants it. She's begging for it and I'm ready to make her take it. I keep her there for what feels like a lifetime. Desperate. Hungry. Moaning my name. Until I shove into her with one final, mighty thrust.

The sensation makes her tighten and collapse into tremors of pleasure. I push her over the edge for the second time and she takes me with her. I ride a tidal wave of pleasure that leaves my whole body convulsing like nothing I've ever experienced.

I grunt my release as I empty myself into her. Kaylee wraps her legs around my back, milking me to the last drop. I collapse onto her. I crush her into the bed and revel in the warm, hazy, afterglow of our mind-blowing sex.

"Can you breathe? I hope so because I never want to move again." My words come out with a strangled chuckle as I try to catch my breath.

"Don't move. Let's live here. Let's stay here like this forever." Kaylee giggles as she traces a finger across the back of my neck.

"Forever," I whisper in agreement. I close my eyes and rest my head on her stomach exhaling all my stress and inhaling the hope for what a future with Kaylee could look like. Being here with her is pure bliss.

Boom. Boom.

Our post-orgasm glow is disrupted by the sound of something slamming into the locked door of the room hard enough to make it rattle on its hinges. Kaylee lets out a scream of stark, unwavering terror, and I all but launch myself off the bed.

Chapter Eight: Kaylee

The sound of something slamming into the door in a hotel that's rumored to be haunted is terrifying and no one's ever accused me of being brave. Shawn rolls and then springs to his feet with impressive agility. He hops around the side of the bed, hands bladed and held in front of his chest like some kind of naked ninja.

Even through my fear, I can't help but let out a giggle at the sight. I sit straight up in bed, eyes wide. But the sound of footsteps on the creaky floors has me rolling off the opposite side of the bed and slamming my shoulder against the old bookcase.

Shawn peers out of the door and into the hall then turns back to me. "Nothing."

"Nothing? It wasn't nothing. I heard the boom and then the sound of walking." My cheeks flush with heat as I scurry to Shawn's side and press myself against his back.

"You're okay, I've got you. But I know what you mean." He takes my hand in his and gives it a gentle squeeze.

But the distinct sound of muffled voices has me swallowing a lump in my throat. "We should get out of here."

"We will, but this is so odd. It sounds like the talking is behind this wall. It's strange because I don't think anything is back there." Shawn runs his hand along the wall touching the gold-framed portrait. When he does, he jumps back. "Oh shit, you can see through the eyes into the lobby by the elevator. This is awesome."

"Oh thank goodness, so it isn't a ghost. I mean, of course, it isn't a ghost." I let out an awkward chuckle. "The detail they put into this place is unbelievable. You're like a sexy, naked spy. What do you see?"

"There isn't anyone out here now, but it looks like there was. The elevator doors just closed." Shawn steps aside. "Here, you can take a look."

I stand on my tiptoes and put my eyes to the painting. Sure as anything, I can see through the tiny holes straight out into the hall. It's such a neat detail.

I gasp when I see the elevator doors open and a man in a suit steps out with one of the bridesmaids tucked into his side. "There are two people getting off the elevator!" Their bodies are pressed together and she looks absolutely smitten. "Ooh, it looks like we aren't the only ones making a love connection tonight. Look at those two. It looks like..." I stop talking and my stomach clenches as the man turns around. "Oh no."

"What's wrong?" Shawn asks.

"Uh, it's..." I frantically search for the words to explain the horror I'm witnessing, but it's no use. There isn't any smoothing this over. I squeeze my eyes shut and shake my head. "It's Spencer."

"He and my sister sneaking off together to do who knows what. Great, just what I want to spend my night thinking about." Shawn lets out a humorless chuckle.

I put my hand on my chest. I might be sick. "No, it's um, it's Spencer but the girl he's with is not your sister." My stomach clenches and I step away from the frame.

In an instant, Shawn is peering through the frame and pounding a clenched fist on the wall. "That son of a bitch. On their wedding night?" He takes a step toward the door.

"No, what are you doing? You're naked!" My voice is almost a shout and still barely seems to register in Shawn's mind.

He turns back to me, his eyes go dark. "Then I'll kill him naked."

I scramble to put myself between Shawn and the door. I don't know if I can stop him, but I know I have to try. Not for his sake, and definitely not for Spencer's, but for Stella. My fellow single mom who deserves a night of peace before the storm she doesn't even know is coming.

"Listen to me. He is an asshole who doesn't deserve your sister or your niece. The only person you have to convince of that is your sister. You beating him up right now isn't going to help your case. You need to calm down. Then you can talk to Kaylee. She's probably in bed anyway, it's almost midnight and it may be her wedding, but she's still a mother to a toddler. She's probably tired. Give her this last moment of peace before you drop a bomb on her entire world."

I know I'm overstepping, but I also know all too well what it's going to do to Stella when she gets the news from her big brother that her husband and the father of her child is slinking around abandoned rooms and getting cozy with one of her bridesmaids. I rest my hand on Shawn's bare chest and his skin is hot to the touch. I can feel his heart beating out of control. But he turns away from the door.

"I don't get it. I hate him, I hate liars. My sister needs to get out of there. Can you imagine starting your life with someone based on a lie?"

I swallow the lump in my throat. "I know what you mean, but sometimes lies in the beginning are—"

"No way, I hate liars. That's something you don't come back from in a relationship." Shawn steps away from the door and starts collecting his clothing.

I know he's not talking about us, or at least I don't think he is. But regardless, the conviction in his tone is enough to make me sick to my stomach. If earlier wasn't the right time to bring up Rosie, the timing now is impossibly worse.

"Here." Shawn tosses my purple tulle zombie dress into a pile on the bed. "Let's head back." His tone is serious.

"Yeah, that's probably a good idea." I agree.

As we make our way across the property and back toward our hotel rooms, Shawn doesn't reach for my hand and I don't offer it either. The energy between us is dramatically more somber than it was a few hours ago.

He's worried about the man telling lies to his sister. I'm worried about being the liar in his life.

When we reach our hotel rooms, I consider whether we'll be sharing a bed tonight. An hour ago, I assumed we would be and I was looking forward to it. But now the mood is completely different and I'm not so sure. But it turns out not to be a problem because Shawn opens the door to my hotel room and walks straight through the adjoining door to his.

"Are you headed to bed?" I ask, my eyes burning.

"You are amazing and you deserve to be with me when I'm at my best. Right now, I can't think about anything other than my sister and I need to deal with this. She deserves to know the truth about why she's sleeping alone on her wedding night in time to get this thing annulled. I need to head over there." His tone is decided and I know there isn't any changing his mind.

"Of course, she's your sister, you know better than anyone what she needs." I swallow hard and think of poor Stella dreaming peacefully. "But just so you know, I don't only want to see you when you're at your best."

Shawn leans in toward me and plants a chaste kiss on my cheek that feels half-hearted at most. When he disappears through the door of the hotel room, I make my way into the bathroom to wash the dramatic makeup off my face and get ready to fall into bed.

I take out my phone and see two missed calls from my sister. My heart rate picks up. I hope everything is alright with Rosie. I glance at the clock, it's after midnight and probably too late to call. I send my sister a text, just in case she's still up.

Me: Hey, sorry I was out. Everything okay with Rosie? Can I call in the morning?

Then the guilt sets in. I'm over here pretending that the most important thing in my life doesn't exist. *What kind of a mother does that?* I've completely lost sight of the fact that this is only a job.

I need a reality check before I get too carried away. Shawn isn't in love with me. How could he be? He doesn't know that my daughter, the most important thing in my entire universe even exists and if he did, he's made it clear he wouldn't want any part of her.

It's selfish of me to be carrying on like this and not only for Rosie's sake. I'm selling Shawn on a life that doesn't exist. A carefree, childfree version of me that will be nothing but another disappointment in his life when he realizes *that me* isn't reality.

My reality is long hours at a bakery and living paycheck to paycheck. My reality is picking out school clothes and helping my daughter with her homework. Then in the precious few hours left in my day, it's recharging my own battery enough to do it all over again in the morning.

It's difficult, but I wouldn't want it any other way. I'm proud of the life I've created, but there isn't any mistaking the fact that I have fought hard for every single thing in my world. I don't want to hide that, not even for a weekend.

Suddenly, my options are clear. I can tell Shawn the truth and watch him decide to hate me for the lie I've carried on for far too long. I can leave without taking a single cent of his money and tell him that we aren't meant to be. Or I can handle this like the business transaction it is, fulfill my obligation until tomorrow, take the cash and hop on my flight never to speak to him again. As I settle into bed, I don't like the way any of these scenarios play out in my mind.

Buzz. Buzz.

My phone vibrates in my hand and it sends me bolting upright. I glance down to see my sister's name illuminated on the screen and I answer the call immediately.

"Hannah, hi. So sorry, is everything okay with Rosie?" I blurt into the phone.

"Mommy?" Rosie's voice echoes on the other end of the line. She sounds sad and it breaks my heart.

"Hi honey, what are you still doing up?" I blink back tears.

"I want you to come home. I can't sleep so Auntie Hannah said I could call you."

"I know honey, I know. It's been a long trip. I'm going to be home tomorrow okay? Why don't you tell me what you two did today?"

"Well, we were walking to the park with Buddy on a leash..."

As Rosie talks, all of my priorities shift back into their proper place and everything becomes clear. By the time we hang up, I know exactly what I need to do. I need to get home to my daughter.

Chapter Nine: Shawn

As my sister peers out of the door at me, she squints into the light. Her face is twisted and her eyebrows are arched. She looks rightfully confused as to why I'm pounding on the door of her hotel room at this hour on her wedding night.

"What's wrong?" Her half-open eyes already have dark circles under them. "If this is about you settling your issue with Spencer, he isn't here, he's out drinking with the guys. And for the record, I'm not mad at you. He deserved the punch and at least the wedding pictures were already taken."

I don't say anything, because now that I'm here, I don't know where to start. Kaylee may have had a point about giving my sister the night to sleep in peace, but it's too late for that now. So I push past Stella and sit on the corner of her bed.

I take a deep breath and brace myself for a gut-wrenching conversation. I know there's a possibility that she won't believe me but this is my little sister and I have to try. I get right to the point.

"Stella, I'm only telling you this because I love you and I can help you. This is terrible and my own feelings about Spencer aside, I hate that I have to say this. Spencer was out walking with... or cozying up to... He was getting out of an elevator arm and arm with one of your bridesmaids. I'm sorry."

I hold my breath and wait for a big response. Maybe shock. Surprise. Anger. Disbelief. But instead, Stella only tilts her head to the side and bites her bottom lip. "Again? Ugh, I figured." She sits onto the bed beside me and pulls her knees to her chest.

"What the hell do you mean again?" My face pinches into tight lines.

"I mean that it's happened so many times I don't have anything left in me. I only feel numb. Let me guess, she was a redhead, Lexi. The one friend who he claims is like a sister to him."

"I don't know what she looked like, I didn't see her. Kaylee did. But sis, if you know, why'd you marry him?"

Stella rolls her neck around as if she's bored. If not for her sighs and the tears I see building behind her eyes, I might actually believe her nonchalance. "McKenna. I had to know that I did everything in my power to give her a normal life with two parents at home. Spencer is a wild card, if we aren't together, he might never make the time to see her. I have to force him to spend time with her as it is. But this isn't the example I want to set for her."

My stomach turns and I'm furious. "That makes me sick. He doesn't deserve to have a wife like you or a daughter as wonderful as McKenna. He doesn't appreciate either of you. I can't make you do anything but I can promise you that I will take care of you and McKenna. I will pay for whatever you need, a house, a lawyer... Get away from him, he's never been good for you. You're worth more than this."

That seems to break the dam. Everything Stella's been holding back comes rushing out. She tells me that being a single parent is terrifying. I remind her that she's already doing it. She tells me that her daughter deserves a family. I remind her that McKenna already has the best family out there.

And then, Stella cries. It's something I've only seen her do a handful of times and it's a heartbreaking sight. I watch as my sister sobs. She tells me that she isn't sad about ending her relationship, only that she's embarrassed to have let it go on this long.

"He is the worst and I can't believe all those jackass things he said about you at the reception. I'm sorry. I messed this one up so badly and now I'm stuck with him all my life or at least for eighteen years because he'll always be McKenna's dad." She puts her face in her hands.

"Yes he will and we'll help him through that. He may surprise us all and rise to the occasion to become a good dad, but he doesn't get to be your husband. So annulling this marriage is a place to start."

"Okay, what do I need to do?"

I saw this coming from day one with Spencer, but I couldn't do anything to stop it. Stella is another name on the list of people I love and cannot keep safe. I look at my strong, capable, sister crumpled into a ball and all I can think is, *this is love.*

This is what love does to you. It makes confident, independent people who have the world at their fingertips turn into... this. Love makes you marry the guy who cheats on you. Love lies to you. Love lets your son get in a car with a drunk man. Love is a gamble and I don't know if it's a bet I'm willing to take again.

Maybe I've already let myself take things too far with Kaylee. Maybe I should have kept our exchange strictly business. But it's too late for that, I've muddied the waters. Should I head back and pay her so we can both move on with our lives or would love be different with her?

I don't want Kaylee's name added to the list of people I can't keep safe. She's too fragile, too good. I don't want her heartache on my hands, not with what she's already been through in her life.

I stay in my sister's room until the sun comes up and we make a plan for her annulment. I send out an email notifying all the guests of the cancellation of the remaining events. I leave a message at my lawyer's office. We make a plan to talk to our parents together.

By the time I head back to my hotel room, my eyes are burning. I crack open the door and wonder whether Kaylee will be in my bed. She isn't. But of course, she isn't and that's probably for the best. I tiptoe over to close the adjoining door when I hear her call out to me.

Chapter Ten: Kaylee

"Shawn?" I blink my eyes open and look into the light pouring in through the door. I'm only half awake and it's disorienting.

"It's me, no worries. I just got back. Sorry I woke you." His voice is weary and all I want is to hug him.

But the discomfort between Shawn and me pales in comparison to what his sister went through today and it's the first thing that pops into my mind. "It's okay, I'm having trouble sleeping anyway. How did it go with your sister?" I can't help but ask.

I have no idea what time it is but even when I was asleep, thoughts of Stella's heartbreak danced in my mind. She's such a good person, a strong single mom like me, and she deserves so much more than what she got from Spencer today.

Shawn steps into my room and sits on the corner of my bed. "Well, the good news is there's no breakfast tomorrow. What a waste of a cool costume, right?" He chuckles humorlessly. "This whole thing is a shit show."

He leans back onto his elbows and for a moment, I think he might climb in bed with me. Even though it would be a stupid decision, a part of me wishes he would. My breath catches in my throat. He pauses and I wonder whether he's thinking about it too. But in the end, he doesn't climb into bed with me. Instead, I put my hand on his back and Shawn stiffens with my touch, so I pull away.

"Listen about earlier—" He starts, but I can't stomach it. Not right now, in the dead of night, on what has already been too long of a day.

So I cut him off. "Love is pretty overrated. We got carried away back there, don't worry about it. I didn't do anything I didn't want to do, but I know it was all just... fun." The words taste bitter as they leave my mouth.

"I don't know if it was all just... fun. I—" Shawn tries to continue, but I stop him again.

"You know what, don't worry about it. It's okay, no offense taken," I reassure him. "You should probably go get some sleep."

"Oh, I see." Shawn gets to his feet and my heart sinks in my chest. "Is everything okay with you?" He sounds so sincere, it breaks my heart.

"Yeah, I'm good. It's been a long weekend and a long night. But I was thinking if there's no breakfast tomorrow, would it be okay with you if I change my flight and head out early?" I burrow down deep under the hotel's heavy comforter, thankful that he can't see my expression in the pitch blackness. "I think it's probably a relief for both of us. You can get back to your real-life and so can I. Hopefully, your sister can have a fresh start at some point too."

"Wow, okay, uh yes. I will make sure you have your money so you can go. You're no longer a hostage in this sick little world of mine." His tone is harsh and cutting but I don't blame him. Heavy tears build behind my eyes.

"It has been a nice weekend. I think we're both tired right now." I make a half-hearted attempt to smooth things over. I don't want to leave things on a bad note. But I don't think now is the right time to tell him about Rosie either.

Shawn takes a few steps toward the door, then he stops and turns back toward the bed. "You know what Kaylee, this bothers me. I'm unsure about taking chances on the idea of love because it seems to end badly for me. But I loved the idea of taking a chance on you. This was real for me, and I'm disappointed to find out that you're just one hell of an actress." His words don't have any bite left in them, only hurt, and it makes me sick to my stomach.

He waits for a response and when he's met with silence, Shawn turns and heads toward the door. I've waited my whole life to meet a man like Shawn and here I am, ruining a good thing. It's like me to do something like this... but it doesn't have to be. My daughter isn't the only person who deserves healthy relationships in her life. I sit straight up in bed.

"Shawn."

"Forget it, you're right. Let's go to bed." When I call his name, he stops and turns back toward me.

I take a deep breath and then swallow my pride and decide to tell the truth whether or not this is the right time. "I'm not any better than Spencer, I've lied to you from the first minute I answered your ad. I have a daughter. Her name is Rosie, and she's young. I'm a full-time mom and my sister is watching her for the weekend so I can be here. Since it seems you have a healthy aversion to having kids, I didn't want to tell you because I need the money. So there you have it, you should go. I'm a liar with a kid. Two things you can't stand."

I can't make out the look on his face in the darkness, but all the air is sucked out of the room and this time it doesn't feel good. Prickles of discomfort tingle on the back of my neck and I exhale. Even though I'm sure he's upset, it feels good to have come clean with Shawn. Where we go from here is only up to him at this point. I've done my part.

He doesn't say anything for a few moments until finally two, strangled, clipped words come out in a soft tone. "You lied?"

"Yes. I did. I know you probably feel tricked, but I was only playing the part you asked me to play. So, I guess I really am one hell of an actress." A lump settles in my throat and a rush of sadness washes over me. Silent tears fall down my face.

I like Shawn more than I'd like to admit. These last few days on his arm have been the happiest of my life. Even if this is the last time I ever see him, I'm better for it. I've always known the way I hoped a man would make me feel and now I have a face to attach to the picture in my mind. And now, he knows the whole truth about me.

"I think I better go." Shawn's tone is unreadable. Is it shock I hear? Disappointment? Frustration? I can't tell. But he keeps walking until he reaches the door then closes it behind him.

I lay silently in the blackness of the hotel room. Things hit differently this early in the morning. They stick around. They run through my brain with no sense of direction, popping in and turning my stomach.

When will I learn that people who grow up like me don't end up in families like Shawn's? I knew better than to let my guard down. Shawn will always be just another great almost.

Another hour passes before the sun is fully in the sky and I give up on sleep completely. Shawn isn't a part of my real life. And it's about time I face the reality that I *do* have a real-life and I think I should get back to it.

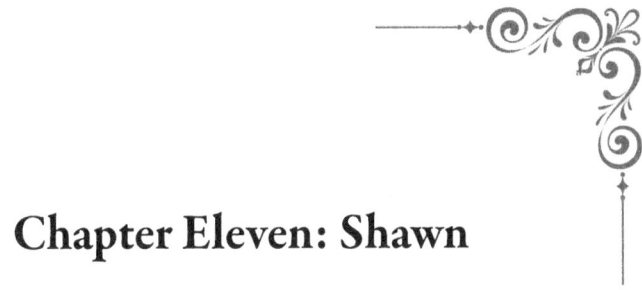

Chapter Eleven: Shawn

I close the door behind me and fall into bed defeated and exhausted. This is love. Every time. It's spectacular until it isn't. The whiplash from the high of being with Kaylee followed by the low of learning it was all a lie makes nausea swirl in my stomach. In the last two days, I've been happier than I have in years. I'm such a fool.

What is the matter with my sister and me? We have two parents who have been madly in love for years. They set an example worth following and yet, Stella will be annulled by the end of the week while I was falling hard for a woman I don't know at all.

Kaylee started our relationship with a lie and it turns my stomach. It isn't just any lie, it's a lie I all but forced her to tell. I gave her a script with a background I thought would suit the situation. I made her dress like a Barbie. How can I fault her for editing the narrative to include one more lie?

I'm not mad at her, I can't be. But of all the things to lie about, why did it have to be that? The simple truth is, I don't think I can be a part of her life because she is a mother. I'm unsure about whether I can keep a heart like Kaylee's safe, but I know for sure I can't be trusted with a child. I've had my chance at being a family man and I failed. That part of my life is over.

I should have known better than to let myself get wrapped up in the fantasy I created. I collapse onto the bed without bothering to change my clothes. All of the events from the last twenty-four hours swirl in my mind creating a dizzying effect. My anger at Spencer. My concern for my sister. My sadness at the realization that Kaylee can't wait to leave.

My eyes burn as I come to the realization that the idea of what could have been between Kaylee and me will haunt me for the rest of my life. When sleep finally comes, it overtakes me like a tidal wave. I dream of Kaylee's smiling face, my hands on her curves, her tits in my mouth. It's pure bliss and I never want to wake up.

TAP. TAP. TAP.

I have been out for what feels like a very long time. But three knocks on my hotel room door have me springing to my feet. In the light of day, and with a clear head, I know I need to talk to Kaylee. I rush to the adjoining door and rip it open.

But when I peer inside, Kaylee's room is vacant. In fact, except for the suitcase in the corner, there isn't any sign of her at all.

Tap. Tap. Tap.

I head to the front door of my hotel room, somehow, I still hope it's her. Maybe she couldn't get into her room. Maybe she felt she had to knock because of the awkward way we left things yesterday. Either way, I hope it's her.

I don't know whether I can get past the fact that she has a kid, or if she even wants me to, but I don't want her to leave before I have a chance to apologize. I pull the door open, ready to pull Kaylee into my arms.

But again, Kaylee isn't anywhere to be found, it's only Stella. My heart sinks in my chest a little.

"Oh, hey sis." I lean on the doorframe.

"Try not to be too disappointed. Were you expecting someone else?" Stella pushes past me with a chuckle and flops into the chair in the corner of my room.

"No, I wasn't expecting anyone." I follow her inside and sit on the corner of the bed. "How are you feeling today?"

"Embarrassed. Like I wasted everyone's time. Sad for McKenna. But also... thankful. I wanted to tell you that hearing you confirm what I've known deep down for a long time was exactly what I needed to finally be done with Spencer. It's messy right now, but it's a good kind of mess. The kind of mess you have to walk through to get to the light on the other side." My sister's eyes go glassy.

"I'm happy to hear that. You'll be okay. Whatever you and McKenna need, I'll make sure it happens." Another swell of rage rises in me at the thought of what Spencer is putting Stella through.

"You know what, I talked to Brandon Brewer last night, Spencer's cousin. It seems his family is just as outraged by Spencer's behavior as we are. Brandon offered me a job here on the property out at the cat cafe. The salary he's giving me is outrageous. Laughable honestly, especially considering what I'll be doing. I know he's only paying me that much because he feels bad but at this point, I have to take it. I couldn't depend on Spencer when we were together, now that he'll move on to create his own life, I have to do what I can to make sure I can take care of my daughter."

As my sister talks, there's a quiet confidence in her tone that's new. Somehow I know that my sister and my niece will be okay. It makes me wonder what the story is with Kaylee and her daughter. Does she have an ex-husband or ex-lover around? Has she done it all on her own? How could I have been so careless in making a show of not wanting kids? How could I have been so selfish with her time? Of course, she wants to leave early, she wants to see her daughter.

I'm lost deep in my own thoughts when I notice Stella isn't talking anymore. She's staring at me, her eyebrows arched up.

"What?" I ask, suddenly wondering if my sister can read my mind.

"You know what I've honestly been thinking? Someday I'm going to find something exactly like what you have with Kaylee. By the way, where *is* Kaylee?"

"Oh, um, she's gone. She left early to head back home." I stand and pull a bottle of water from the mini-fridge.

"I really like her. My wedding weekend was a bust but the best thing to come out of it was getting to meet Kaylee. She's fantastic, and such a natural with kids. McKenna loves her and I can tell you do too. I haven't seen you this happy in a long time." Stella's words sting and the muscles in my jaw tighten.

Impulsively, I decide to come clean. "I lied. I hired Kaylee to be my date to prove to you all and to myself that I have moved on past the horrors that have haunted me in this town."

"What are you talking about?" Stella's mouth falls open in shock as I continue my confession.

I don't hold back. I give her the details. I tell her about the made-up backstory and the way Kaylee memorized every word. I tell her how I didn't expect to fall in love, but I'm on my way nonetheless. I tell her about the way Kaylee makes me feel like the man I want to be. When I stop talking, my sister's eyes look like they might pop out of her head.

I finish off the bottle of water. "I know, it's terrible, right?"

"What's terrible about it? I don't care how Kaylee got here, all that matters is that she's here now and you two are fantastic together." Stella sits up straight.

"There's something else... She has a kid she didn't tell me about." The words are heavy when they slip out of my mouth and hang in the air between us. "Well, I guess that isn't fair. She didn't tell me about her daughter because I told her I didn't want kids... I made kind of a *thing* of it." Admitting it aloud makes me uncomfortable.

"Just when I thought I couldn't love her any more than I already do." Stella's face stretches into a broad smile and I shake my head, trying to make sense of her reaction. "Shawn, you lost your son, you're a dad without a kid, and it isn't your fault. You should be a dad again, the world needs more good ones and you are one of the best." Stella makes her proclamation with so much conviction, I want to believe it too.

"I've forgiven myself for not being there to protect my family all those years ago, but I assumed that was the end of my story. I never thought that I might get a second chance at being a parent. I like Kaylee, I might even love her already. But there's so much I don't know about her and obviously, I haven't met her daughter at all. I don't even know how old she is." My heart rate ticks up as I realize what's at stake.

"Well then what are you doing here with me? You've got to find her. Go ask her every question you can think of and don't let her go." Stella shrugs like I'm the dullest person she's ever met.

"Okay, yeah. That's exactly what I'll do." I get to my feet and collect my wallet and phone. "You and McKenna don't need anything?" I can't help but ask.

"We need a chance at having Kaylee in our lives and having Uncle Shawn back to his old self. Now hurry up and go." Stella smirks at me.

"Thanks, sis." I tear out of the doorway and down the hall.

Chapter Twelve: Kaylee

The cool mountain air feels good as it fills up my lungs. I've been hiking around the Brewer property all morning trying to get a hold of myself. As I pause to take a sip of water, I settle against a boulder and take my phone from my bag. I'm happy to see that I now have reception.

I've been in my own head, marveling at my own odd behavior. The way I've been behaving is so strange for me, waltzing around like I don't have a care in the world. But today that ends, I'm flying back home. I dial my sister, talking to Hannah is exactly what I need to ground myself back in the realities of my daily life.

"Hello there!" Hannah's voice is chipper as usual.

"Hey Hannah, how is everything? Rosie doing okay this morning?" I wipe the sweat from my brow.

"Yes, she's totally fine. She only needed to hear your voice. She slept like a baby and now she's running out back with the pups. Want me to grab her for you?"

"No, that's okay. If she's happy I don't want to interrupt." My stomach swirls.

"You on the other hand sound... off. How are things with you and Mr. Perfectly plastic?"

As soon as Hannah asks the question I'm reminded that my sister knows me too well for me to even consider pretending. So I answer her honestly.

"Ugh, I don't know. Shawn is so good, so sweet, but I think I let myself get wrapped up in this fantasy. He doesn't know about Rosie and I haven't told him on purpose. But with things between us... as they are now, I wish I had told him from the beginning. It doesn't matter at this point I guess... anyway, the good news is I'm getting back on a plane in a few hours so I'll be home early."

"No, no, no. I'm not accepting that weird summary. Tell me exactly what happened." Hannah isn't planning on letting me off the hook and truthfully I'm fine with it.

I know myself and I need to talk it out just as much as Hannah needs to hear the details. I continue my hike back toward the hotel. When I round the bend on the trail and see the Brewer property out in the distance, I know I'm not ready to be back yet. So I let myself pause, leaning against a tree. I take a deep breath and without another moment of hesitation, I tell Hannah everything.

I tell her that I've fallen for Shawn and his entire family. I tell her about Stella and the way she stood up for herself. I tell her about the mind-blowing sex and the way Shawn held me afterward.

I tell Hannah that for a moment, I believed all of it. That I thought my life, Rosie's life, and somehow, Hannah's life, were about to be turned on their axis. I thought maybe it was love between me and the thoughtful, sexy, sincere man who made me feel like I was the only person in the world who matters. Hannah gasps with each new revelation and I let myself smile as I talk about Shawn.

But then I explain the gut-wrenching realization that none of this can mean anything because Shawn doesn't want kids. He doesn't know about the biggest part of my life and he already doesn't like it. I tell her that I lied to him in the beginning and then continued the lie beyond what is reasonable. I tear up when I tell Hannah about Shawn's son and his ex-wife.

Getting all of it out of my head and into the world feels good. As I say the words, they seem to organize themselves into logical thoughts.

The blur of emotions fades and shifts before sharpening into straight lines.

"When it comes down to it, I can't be with anyone who doesn't see Rosie as a gift. She's my whole world and if Shawn has to be convinced of that, he isn't the person for me. It's that simple... it has to be. It's too bad because I think, or at least I thought there could be so much more between us." My breathing slows and the sweat feels cold as it runs down my back.

"I get that, believe me... but can I ask why you think he doesn't understand that? I know he said he didn't want kids and after his tragic past, I can't blame him. But do you think there's a chance he felt blindsided by the fact that Rosie exists at all?" Leave it to my sister to force me to push my boundaries as soon as I set them.

"I suppose." Even though she can't see me, I put a defensive hand on my hip as we talk.

"I know you don't want to hear this, but maybe you should talk to him about it. You know, in the light of day. When he hasn't been up for twenty-four hours fighting his future-ex-brother-in-law." Hannah chuckles into the phone and I already know she's right.

Don't I owe Shawn at least that much? A conversation? The whole truth?

"It wasn't much of a fight," I laugh. "Shawn obliterated him with a single punch. It was pretty satisfying. Spencer is the worst."

My sister asks for details about every single person at the wedding including their costume choices and personalities. I tell her about my time with McKenna and how I can imagine her and Rosie being the best of friends. I tell her that I'm disappointed I never had the chance to wear the third costume Shawn picked out for me.

By the time my sister and I hang up, it's obvious what I need to do. I need to find Shawn and clear the air. Even if it isn't us at the end of this, the fact is, I'm happy I came. Shawn was who I needed to restore my faith in men and to give me hope that maybe I'll find my own happily ever after one day. But if I'm being honest, I *want* it to be us.

I make my way back into my hotel room and go straight to the adjoining door without bothering to change or shower. Maybe I should put myself together first, but this conversation can't wait. I tap lightly three times and when I don't hear anything in response, I crack the door open. I peek inside my breath held shallow in my chest.

But it's all for nothing. The room is vacant. Shawn isn't here.

What if I missed my chance to make things right with him? What if he doesn't want anything to do with me? What if there isn't any coming back from the lie?

Sadness swirls in my stomach. My heart hurts but I'm not ready to give up. I pull out my phone to send Shawn a text message. I'll apologize. I'll ask him if he wants to talk. But before I can, I notice a white envelope sitting on top of my bag with my name scrawled across the front.

There's a knot over my chest that makes it hard to breathe. It's going to be the money, I know it. The envelope is proof that this, all of it, was a business transaction for Shawn and nothing more. Having enough money in this envelope to secure my daughter's education somehow doesn't feel as good as I thought it would.

I swallow the lump in my throat as I take the thick envelope in my hands and tear the top open. But when I peer inside, there isn't any cash to be found. I'm surprised to find nothing but a card. When I pull it out, it looks more like a formal invitation than a check.

Dear Kaylee,

You are the kind of woman who deserves to be taken on a real date. I'd like to be the man who gets to do that with you. I have it all planned out. If you're willing to give me a chance to redeem myself after my shameful reaction to the wonderful news about you being a mother, please meet me out front by the fountain at one. If not, know that I won't stop trying.

*You've awakened something in me that I didn't even know existed and I
don't want to let you go.*

Xoxo,

Shawn

P.S. Wear the costume.

Excitement whips through me and once I've recovered from the
shock of the invitation, I don't pause to give it a second thought.
Instead, I throw my suitcase on the bed and unzip it. I pull everything
out and search for the only costume I haven't worn yet. Once it's laid
out, I race through a shower.

I check the time as I step out of the shower and into my slutty
vampire outfit. It fits like it was made for me. It accentuates my curves
and it must have cost a small fortune. The black and purple tulle of
the skirt hardly covers my ass. Even I have to admit the sequin on the
excessively tight corset makes my chest look fantastic as I lace it up. The
tall, black boots and fishnet tights paired with the cape top off the look.

I pin the front of my hair back and spray it into place. Then I apply
a healthy coat of burgundy lipstick, false lashes, and contouring that
makes me look undead. When I apply my final coat of black eyeliner, I
can't help but wonder what it is Shawn has in store for me. Not that it
matters, seeing him is all I need.

An hour later, I'm flying through the lobby and out of the hotel's
front doors. My cape flaps in the breeze behind me. I'm a bundle of
nervous excitement, quick breath, shaking hands, and a giddy smile.

I step outside and the crisp autumn air washes over me. I inhale
through my nose and take it all in. I want to remember this moment
because I just know that this is the moment before my life changes.
Not because Shawn is going to save me, but because he might run away
from his life and into mine. I slow my breath and walk to the circular
fountain at the front of the entrance of the hotel.

I look around expectantly. At first glance, Shawn isn't anywhere to
be found. But then, I spot it and my eyes light up. There's a golf cart

approaching in the distance. As it gets closer, I see it's covered in purple fairy lights and draped in black mosquito netting secured with sequin bows. The driver is the sexiest vampire I've ever seen and all I can think is, *step aside Edward Cullen.*

Butterflies flap in my stomach. When Shawn stops the cart in front of me, he hops out with a bouquet of purple roses in his hand. The black shirt he has on clings to every one of the muscles in his chest and I can't pull my eyes away.

"You came." Shawn holds out his arms to me and I sink into them. He holds me tight, pinning my head to that perfect spot on his chest and I breathe him in. When he pulls away, I look up at him. His eyes are dark and crackling with warmth. "These are for you."

"Thank you, they're beautiful... and of course I came." I can't stop the truth from spilling out. "Shawn I'm sorry I lied. I needed the money from your job listing to put my daughter into private school. She's the best thing that's ever happened to me and I love her with all my heart. I want her to have a better life than I did. I'm raising her on my own and I don't make a ton of money at the bakery. That's it, the whole truth. Everything else I told you was true. The way I feel about you is real. I hope you can see that."

"I know sweetheart." Shawn runs his hand up and down my back. "I can see that. I shouldn't have reacted the way I did, I was wrong. I'm sorry I made you feel bad even for a moment. My son was one of my favorite people on the planet. I can't imagine how I would have felt if anyone saw him as anything less. If I'm ever lucky enough to meet your daughter, I'd be the happiest man. Maybe it's something we can work toward."

Tears fill my eyes as Shawn says every word I never knew I was desperate to hear. "It's something to work toward." I nod and choke my words out through tears of joy.

"For now I'm satisfied with getting to be the guy who gets to take you on a real date, albeit a spooky one. Sorry, I couldn't get a limo on such short notice, so this is your chariot for the day." He holds out his hand to me and when I take it, he helps me into the golf cart.

"I can't believe you did this, it's perfect." I giggle and admire the bouquet of flowers as Shawn gets into the driver's seat. "But you know, you really shouldn't make a habit of joyriding in this thing."

Shawn smirks at me with one eyebrow raised as he starts the engine. He bumps us right through the center of the golf course and out of the other side. He holds my hand as we drive past the pub on the property and doesn't slow until we arrive way out at the greenhouses.

"Are we supposed to be out here?" I ask.

"Yeah, the Brewers have given me Spencer to deal with for the rest of my life, letting me borrow the space out here for our date was the least they can do," Shawn chuckles.

"Fair enough," I giggle.

Shawn takes my hand to the back of his mouth and kisses it. "I have so many plans for us, but this seemed like a good place to start. Now, I know there isn't a door for me to open for you, but don't you dare get out until I come around."

"Promise."

My heart beats fast as I watch Shawn hop out of the driver's seat and make his way around to my side of the golf cart. He might be the only person who can pull off what is essentially a too-small shirt tucked into black pleather pants with a cape, but the man is doing it so well it makes my mouth water.

Shawn holds his elbow out to me and escorts me to the greenhouse in the center with the open doors. When we step inside, I gasp.

The space is stunning. There are illuminated candles on every surface and they bounce warm shades of light in every direction. The plants are moved to the perimeter and in the center of the room is a table set for two complete with white a linen tablecloth, black place settings, and a bottle of white wine on ice. On the table is a bouquet made of dark purple roses with vibrant green accents.

The room is breathtaking. It seems too good to be true. It's a fairytale, a scene from a book. It's everything I love about Halloween, only better. This date is all treat with no trick. Shawn is a perfect gentleman. He pulls out my chair and pushes it in behind me as I sit. He pours me a glass of wine. I feel so taken care of, so valued.

"I'm shocked, you have outdone yourself. This is incredible." I reach across the table and put my arm on his, heat bubbles between us. "I can't believe you did all this for me. You know what, Rosie loves Halloween as much as I do. She'd think this was incredible."

"Does she?" Shawn stares at me, intensity darkening his eyes.

"What? Is it weird to think of me as a mother all of a sudden?" I can't help but ask.

"No, that isn't it at all. There was something maternal about you from the moment I saw you, you were so natural with McKenna. I was thinking that I can't believe that there's a man out there in this world who is stupid enough to have had you and let you go without so much as taking you on a proper date. What an idiot." Shawn shakes his head in disgust.

"He kind of is an idiot." I can't help but chuckle. "But truthfully, it was never going to work between us, we were young and stupid. The difference is, I grew up when I became a mother, he never did. But he had to be out of the picture so that I could end up here with you now and that feels worth it."

"It's my honor. I wanted to take you somewhere special, but I couldn't find anywhere that screamed Kaylee, so I made a place just for us. I needed a place with plants and candles. Somewhere spooky, but not scary. And... here, take a look." Shawn hands me a menu.

When I open it, I squeal with excitement. "Shawn, it's perfect! There isn't a single item that doesn't have sugar as its primary ingredient," I giggle.

"Correct, I've been listening. All desserts." He winks at me and raises his glass in my direction.

I stew over the menu and marvel at how much thought went into crafting it. All of my favorites are listed. In the end, when our server appears, I order a pumpkin cheesecake. Shawn goes with the scone.

While we eat, he insists on asking me all the first date questions, even the ones he already knows the answers to. He tells me my responses sit differently now that I'm here by choice and not because I'm being paid. Shawn and I fall into easy, winding, conversation as if we've been together all our lives.

As we wrap up our meal, I gaze at him from across the table. "You are amazing, this is too much. It's everything I never thought I'd have."

"You deserve everything. You're incredible. I haven't smiled so much in years. There's one more thing I need to ask you." Shawn fumbles with his phone and music pipes into the greenhouse from a speaker I can't see.

It's an airy, instrumental song. It only takes me a second to realize that it isn't just any song, it's my favorite song.

Shawn gets to his feet and holds a hand out to me. "May I have this dance?"

I blush and place my hand in his. Shawn holds on tight and pulls me to my feet. He nestles in close to me and I rest my head on his shoulder as we sway to the music. Our bodies meld together so tight, it's hard to tell where I end and he begins.

His hand starts on my lower back, then makes its way down to my waist and below. It doesn't stop roaming until it lands on the swell of my ass. The sensation sends tingles whipping through me. I feel him stiffen and swell through his costume and it makes me ache for him.

The melody in the tiny glass room has a way of capturing every emotion circling around us. The joy of the moment. The new hope for what a future between us might look like. Pure unadulterated desire.

In an instant, Shawn is all I can see. Our lips crash together and they don't part. From there, it's a frenzied blur of tugging and pulling.

It's capes on the floor. It's me dropping to my knees with his hands in my hair. It's feeling him clench as I bring him to the edge.

It's him winding me up and back down again, claiming my body as his own. Making me moan his name through clenched teeth. It's hard and fast. It's gentle and all-consuming. It's my first date with my forever love.

Chapter Thirteen: Shawn

Two Weeks Later

My stomach bubbles with excitement as I wait by the baggage claim carousel for Kaylee and Rosie to get off their flight. Kaylee and my sister Stella have developed quite a friendship and my parents have been desperate to see more of Kaylee and me, so meeting back in Misty Mountain seemed right.

I'm so grateful that Kaylee is entrusting me with an introduction to her daughter. But I'm not nervous the way I thought I would be because it doesn't feel rushed. In fact, I couldn't imagine going another minute without knowing the little girl that holds Kaylee's heart so tightly.

In the last two weeks, Kaylee and I have talked on the phone every morning, every night, and sent text messages every moment in between. We have the kind of connection that is bigger than the two of us. We bring out the best in one another. She's smart, thoughtful, and sexy as hell.

Memories of the night I spent ravishing her perfect body at the Brewer hotel dance in my head. Every day I'm convinced that I couldn't possibly fall any harder for her and yet with each conversation, I love her more.

My eyes flick across every person coming down the escalator until finally, I see them. Kaylee is in a brown sweater that accentuates her eyes and dark jeans. Rosie is wearing an orange dress and her hair is tied into pigtails. I love seeing Kaylee as a mother.

Kaylee grins at me then leans down and whispers into her daughter's ear, pointing toward me. Rosie follows her line of sight and when her eyes land on mine, she waves wildly. I can't help but chuckle at the sight of her adorable blonde head bobbing up and down. Rosie's definitely got her mother's confidence. I feel so incredibly lucky to be the person on the receiving end of those smiles.

When they reach me, I hug Kaylee and kiss her on the forehead. Holding her, I feel like my life is falling back into place. "Hi beautiful, I've missed you."

"I missed you too." Kaylee's voice is soft and she looks up at me from underneath dark lashes, the corner of her mouth pulls up into a smile. "Shawn, this is my daughter Rosie."

"Hi there, you have no idea how happy I am to meet you," I say. Not wanting to make her uncomfortable, I hold out my hand to her.

Rosie wraps her little fingers around mine and pulls herself toward me. Then she throws her arms around my leg and squeezes. Memories of my son come flooding back to me, but they aren't the sad ones. In her hug, I can feel his smile, hear the honesty in his laugh and the sincerity in his voice.

She pulls away and beams up at me. I feel my heart shift to make room for this little person who doesn't have my eyes but was somehow destined to be mine. Standing with Kaylee and Rosie, I have everything. These two have my whole heart for as long as they'll take it.

BY THE AFTERNOON, ROSIE has negotiated her way into a playdate with McKenna. My sister Stella is all too happy to babysit while I take Kaylee on a date. But when I ask Kaylee where she wants to go, the only place either of us can think of is to bed.

When I get her alone in our hotel room, I kiss Kaylee senseless. I claim her body like it already belongs to me, worshiping her curves, and making her moan my name. As she writhes against me, I already know that no matter how much time we spend here, it'll never be long enough.

We make love for hours. Making good on all the late-night promises we made each other on our phone calls in the last two weeks. We're insatiable. Drenched in sweat. Desperate for each other.

When we take a break, Kaylee lays on her side in front of me, naked, panting, and recovering. I put my arm around her and pull her body into mine. "Can I tell you something?"

She looks up at me, glowing, perfect. "Anything."

"I'm going to marry you. Someday. When you're ready, I'm going to get to be your husband. I know it's soon and maybe now you think I'm crazy, but I don't care. I can feel it." I whisper my words into her ear and trail my fingertips down the length of her body.

Kaylee looks at me, her eyes wide and sparkling. Then she breathes in a long exhale through her nose. "You know what? I think you're right."

Epilogue: Kaylee

One Year Later

The music starts and everyone in the chapel springs to their feet, turning to face the back of the chapel. Rosie and McKenna stand hand in hand wearing adorable white dresses made of tulle. The girls clutch their baskets of flowers and smile nervously at each other.

The chapel at Brew by Brewer makes a beautiful setting for a wedding between two of the most beautiful people I know. The intricate stained glass windows paired with rustic exposed beams and bouquets of fresh floral make for a stunning sight.

I clutch my bridesmaid's bouquet and smile at Shawn from across the altar. Last year we were in this same chapel, waiting for the same bride to make her way down the aisle. But everything else about this wedding is different.

For starters, there aren't any costumes. But more importantly, it seems everyone in the room is at peace with this union. Shawn and I are different too, we don't have to pretend to be in love this time.

I'm so happy for Stella. She's starting her new life in the same place her old one ended and doing it with such grace. As I watch my sister-in-law take her first steps down the aisle, I'm transported back to a few months ago when it was my turn to wear the white dress.

My sister Hannah walked me down the aisle and Shawn cried when he saw me coming. During our ceremony Shawn made vows to love me, to stand beside me, and to always be my home. Then he turned to Rosie and promised to protect her all her life.

I can't help the tears that trickle down my cheeks when I hear Stella's new husband make the same promises to McKenna. Seeing two little girls with strong men who choose to love them as their own makes happiness bubble and swell inside of me. Shawn is the dad Rosie deserves. I'll never stop being in love with their love story. McKenna will grow up knowing her value.

As the officiant pronounces the couple as husband and wife, the happy couple seals their vows with a kiss and the crowd erupts into cheers. A smile pulls at Shawn's face as he watches his sister in the trustworthy arms of her new husband.

When it's our turn to exit the chapel, Shawn holds out his elbow to me and I slip my arm through. My heart pounds in my chest the same way it has since the moment I met him. Life by Shawn's side is more than I ever dreamed of.

In the past year, my life has changed exponentially. Shawn, McKenna, Hannah, and I have relocated to Misty Mountain where we live a life rich in family. I've found a job working at the cat cafe on the Brewer property and made new friends along the way. Being here in the crisp mountain air is the fresh start all of us needed.

But more than any of the physical changes, I've grown emotionally. Shawn and I have healed each other in a way I didn't know was possible. We spend our days laughing and our nights dreaming. It's a kind of bliss I've never felt before and I don't take a single minute of it for granted.

Immediately following the ceremony, Shawn and I meet the bride and groom in the garden for a champagne toast with the rest of the bridal party. When they offer me a flute, I take it knowing I can't drink it, and then raise an eyebrow at Shawn. He winks back at me.

Shawn clears his throat. "Sis, before we do this toast, Kaylee and I want you to open your gift." He takes a tiny gold package out from behind the table and hands it to Stella.

"What is this? It better not be anything crazy, I told you two not to go over the top." Stella looks from Shawn to me but I only shrug.

She unwraps the package and unfolds the tissue paper inside until finally, she holds up the tiny blue onesie. "Boy aunt." Stella's voice breaks as she reads the shirt and happy tears build behind her eyes. "You're pregnant?"

I nod as she comes around the table for a hug.

"I'm so happy," she whispers.

Then, Stella turns to her brother. "Shawn, you're going to be a dad again. It's all I've ever wanted for you."

The three of us embrace and I'm overwhelmed with a sense of calm. This baby will come into the world immeasurably loved. He and Rosie will live a life that Hannah and I could have never imagined and it's all because of the handsome man standing beside me.

We raise our glasses and toast to the happy couple. Then I put my arms around Shawn and look up into his pooling eyes. "Thank you for this life we're building together. Thank you for loving me."

Shawn looks down at me, a brilliant, dazzling, smile on his face. "Sweetheart, you, Rosie, and this baby are my happily ever after."

Merry, Chapter One:
Roman

When I took the job as a property manager for the Brew by Brewer resort, I had no idea what I was getting myself into. When I met with the Brewer family, they didn't seem to know either.

In general, it's my job to make sure things keep working. With a property this big, that's no small task. Between the hotel, pub, golf course, brewery, and cat cafe, there's always something that needs fixing.

With each passing year, I'm more and more grateful for my position. This place and the people in it have become something of a surrogate family for me. I keep to myself, make my own hours, and I get to help people. It's ideal.

Christmas is just around the corner and for once, things seem to have slowed a bit. So this morning, I'm taking the opportunity to crunch through the snow out to the back forty and take in the tree line. The view from this part of the mountain is stunning.

The frosty air chills me to my core and I can see my breath as I walk. Moving here, starting over... it's been good for me.

"Hey!" A small voice echoes off the quiet snow. "Sir! Excuse me! Hey!"

I turn to follow the sound over to our cat cafe in the distance. As usual, there is a gaggle of customers inside. The cafe fosters cats who are available for adoption and sometimes, the little furballs draw in quite the crowd. There are certainly a lot of people today, but I can't tell where the voice is coming from.

As I get closer, I spot a little girl with huge eyes and two ponytails standing on the cafe's covered porch. She's tiny, maybe five years old, maybe seven? I haven't spent much time around kids so it's hard to say. But to my surprise, she's staring right at me.

As I get closer, the girl waves to me, flashing her gapped-tooth smile. I double-check behind me just to be sure I'm not missing anything, but I am the only one out here.

When I reach the porch, the girl clears her throat and gives me a thumbs-up. "Excuse me, sir, your table is ready."

"What?"

"Come on, you're sitting in our snow section. Don't worry, we do have a heater, it won't be so cold and I think I can turn it on." The girl looks up at the propane heater. Then drags a chair toward it and I lunge into action.

"No, no sweetheart. I don't think kids are supposed to touch those. They could be dangerous." With no kids of my own and not a whole lot of experience with anyone else's, I'm out of sorts and not sure what to say.

"It's fine, I work here." She puts a hand on her hip.

I bite back a laugh. "Is that so? How old are you anyway?"

"Well, I'm six but soon, I'll be seven and then eight and before you know it I'll be like... ten." She tilts her chin up with pride. "All I need is a customer. You sit and I will start a fire." She gestures to the heater.

"No deal. Where are your parents?"

She points to the cafe and I glance inside. Normally I don't make it out to this part of the property while I'm on shift and now I see why. It's packed. Wall to wall people take over the dining room.

I'm sure this kid's parents are in there somewhere. But for now, I suppose I can do my part by keeping her from playing with the propane heater.

"Are you going to sit? How can I take your order if you don't sit?" She blinks at me, clipboard in hand.

When I plop down on the chair, the little girl's mouth curls into a grin. In all my time working on this property, I've never experienced anything quite like this.

"Okay. I'm McKenna and I'll be your server. Now I have gingerbread men, wreath cookies, something that's green but it always looks gross. I think it's soup." She scrunches her nose and shakes her head. "Or hot chocolate or I think coffee. What would you like to order? Or I can surprise you with the Christmas tree cookies." The adorable kid folds her hands under her chin and rocks onto her tiptoes.

"Um, you can surprise me."

"Okay," McKenna takes a tiny pink notebook out of her back pocket. "How do you spell surprise?"

The wooden door on the front of the cafe pushes open ever so slightly. A white cat with a red and green collar saunters out onto the porch, wrapping herself between my legs.

"Carole Cat! If you're out here, who's flipping the pancakes?" McKenna lets out a laugh at her own joke. "Ugh, it's so hard to find good help! Okay, it's okay. You're a nice cat. I'm not mad." McKenna drops to her knees and scoops the cat into her arms. "Okay sir, we'll be right back with your order." McKenna drops the clipboard and notebook. Then she whips in through the front door of the cafe.

As I sit on the patio, I notice the marked change in my body. My heart rate has slowed, and my mind is undoubtedly present which is a rarity for me. Typically spontaneity has the opposite effect on me.

I never feel this relaxed. Even at night when I should be sleeping, I'm prone to bad dreams and flashbacks. But something about the innocence of this exchange with McKenna has my chest feeling lighter than it has in years. I think I should start visiting the cat cafe more often.

When the door opens again, McKenna is carrying a tray that must weigh more than she does. It's stacked high with cookies, cupcakes, and a still steaming teapot. I spring to my feet.

"Hey, careful." I take the tray from her and put it on the table. "Are you sure you're supposed to be taking those? How in the world did you get past all those people with this massive thing?"

"I told you I work here. So, what do you do?" The little girl raises her eyebrows at me and slides into the chair across from me.

"I uh, I work here. I fix things most of the time, help people, that sort of thing." I shake my head. I can't believe I'm being interrogated by a six-year-old.

"Great, there are so many things I need help with!" McKenna shoves a piece of cookie into her mouth.

"Is that so?" I reluctantly pull the corner off a croissant and when it melts in my mouth, I sit back into my chair.

"First, reading. Also, I need help pouring the tea because it's too hot. Also, do you fix things in other places besides here? Because I have a few things at home you could fix too. I have a playhouse that I can't even play in. My dad dropped it off at my mom's house and he didn't even set it up. She said she can do it but..." McKenna clenches her teeth together and shakes her head.

I have to laugh at this little girl's tenacity. I don't know where she came from, but I can tell her parents are doing something right.

The door to the cafe flies open again and a tall, curvy woman steps out onto the porch wearing a black, Brewer Cat Cafe apron.

Well, hello.

She's striking with her dark eyes, olive skin, and long, glossy hair. The woman's head turns on a swivel until her gaze lands on McKenna. "There you are, I was worried. I told you to watch Carole Cat and then you were just gone. McKenna, that isn't okay. We've talked about you running off before. And..." The woman seems to notice me for the first time. "And what are you doing out here?"

"Mom! We are lunching!"

"Who are you?" The woman's voice is cutting when she turns to me, eyes squinted, and finger pointed.

I get to my feet and hold out my hand to her. "I'm Roman Stony. I'm a property manager here. I was just walking the back half of the resort and McKenna flagged me down."

"McKenna, we don't flag down random dudes. Come on." She shakes her head then puts her hand in mine. "I'm Stella Willman it's nice to meet you. I've been working here for a few weeks now."

Her touch sends tingles crackling through me. The way her face washes with a red flush makes me wonder whether she feels them too.

"I was wondering why I hadn't seen you around yet. Welcome, it's a nice place to work. The Brewer family is one of the best," I say.

"I'm a Brewer too!" McKenna chimes in.

"Yes, this is my daughter, McKenna Brewer. Her father, my ex, Spencer Brewer isn't in the picture. So his family is letting me work here. I have to agree that they are very good people.... Mostly." Stella bites back a laugh and her mouth pulls into a smirk.

Realization dawns. The story of the Halloween-themed wedding that ended in chaos is practically a legend around here. Spencer is a bad dude. I've dealt with him off and on since starting here.

When I heard about his ill-fated wedding, I wondered what kind of woman would have the guts to take on someone like him. Now that I'm standing across from her, it all makes sense. Stella's out of his league and I think she knows it.

She's beautiful, anyone could see that. But there's an intensity in the way Stella talks that draws me in, I find myself wanting to know everything about her. McKenna on the other hand stretches and lets out an exaggerated yawn, seemingly bored to tears with our conversation.

"Mom, Roman fixes things. Can he come over and fix my playhouse? Can I have more of these cupcakes to make a stack? Can I eat one? Can we adopt a cat? We don't have any pets. I want to have a friend at home. I want to go home, I'm so bored here…"

Stella blows out a breath. "You can head inside and see if there are dishes you can help wash."

"Mom, that's fine, but can—" McKenna starts.

"Go," Stella cuts her off.

McKenna throws her head back in a dramatic protest and then disappears into the cafe with Carole Cat in her arms. When it's just the two of us, Stella's demeanor shifts in a small almost imperceptible way. She leans in toward me. She smiles more.

"Thank you for being so patient with her. You must be a parent too."

"No actually, I'm not. Truthfully, it's better that way." I let out a chuckle. Stella can't possibly know how true my statement is.

"I don't believe that. I mean, you just had a tea party in the snow." She tucks a strand of hair behind her ear. "I normally don't bring her with me to work but her dad didn't show up to grab her for the weekend and then my sitter canceled on me again. She's pretty much the worst." Stella's face turns a shade of pink as she rambles. "So here we are."

"Well, lucky me." I shove my hands in my pockets. I shouldn't be flirting with her, but I can't help myself.

Boom. Crash.

The sounds coming from inside the cafe make Stella jump and when I turn to peer in through the window, the source of the chaos is front and center. The large Christmas tree that once stood in the middle of the cafe is flat on its side. Ornaments splay out across the tile floor.

Carole Cat unapologetically pops her head up from the chaos, gives her paw a lick, and then makes her way through the crowd.

"Oh my gosh, this is the third time this week. She can't leave the tree alone, and she isn't even sorry about it! How is she going to be adopted by Christmas if she keeps not caring about impressing our customers? When she finds her forever family, we're going to have to adopt her out with a disclaimer."

"It sounds to me like the problem is the tree, not the cat. I can come inside and take a look," I say.

"No, that's okay. There are so many people in there right now. It's my fault, I just wanted to make it look like Christmas in here but I had that thing balanced on a tiny stand. We'll push it up against the wall or something." The cold turns the tip of her nose a light pink.

"I'll get you set up for now and then when it's less crowded, I'll find a more permanent solution. After you." I hold open the door.

Stella's pillowy pink lips mesmerize me as she steps inside. "Okay, thanks."

I can't tell if it's the Christmas music being piped in through the speakers, the delicious smells, or the fact that Stella is the most charming woman I've ever met but I don't want to leave. So, I don't.

Instead of making my usual rounds across the property, I spend the afternoon at the cat cafe. I build a scratching post for the cats. I tighten loose shelves. I let McKenna hammer in nails for me. I try every item in the cooler.

I fix, help, and laugh my way through the next three hours and it still isn't enough. Stella is warm and engaging. She's a good mom, the kind of person that draws you in and McKenna is a total crack up.

By the time I leave, I'm already wracking my brain to think of reasons to return to the cat cafe. But in the end, the only one I come up with is Stella.

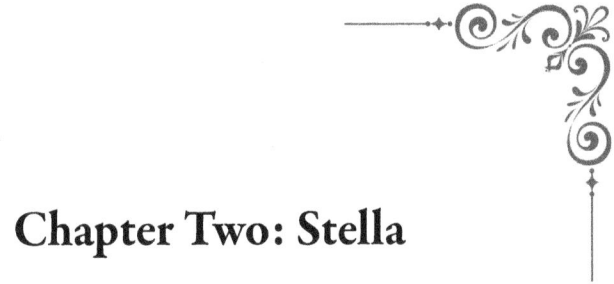

Chapter Two: Stella

Four days have passed since Roman first made his debut into my world. I haven't stopped thinking about him since. I'd guess we are around the same age but there's something old-fashioned about him.

He carries himself with a true air of confidence that's hard to come by these days. When Roman walks in, he makes life better. Takes care of everything. Gets shit done. It's so refreshing.

Plus at two-hundred-sixty pounds of pure muscle, the man isn't bad to look at. He oozes sex appeal. It's distracting. It's unfair for one person to be so perfect. I have no choice but to be just a little giddy when he stops in. Anyone would be.

Each day since our initial meeting, I find myself watching out of the big windows of the cafe. I wait, secretly hoping to see him crunching through the snow in the distance, making his way toward me. Then when he comes through the door, it's all I can do to calm the butterflies in my stomach.

Is it what I should be doing? Of course not.

With Sophia Brewer and Lucy Brewer both out on a tandem maternity leave, the Brewer cat cafe has been left in the capable hands of Kaylee, my brother Shawn's new girlfriend.

I love her to pieces and I want to make sure I'm doing my part to help things run smoothly while she's in charge. Besides, when Spencer bailed on McKenna and me, Brandon Brewer offered to pay me an astronomical amount of money to work here. Baking and fostering adorable kittens isn't a bad life.

Even though I knew I was a total charity case, I took the position. I work as hard as I can to show him that I appreciate it. Making my own money has allowed me to be an example of independence for my daughter and that means everything to me.

I pull my tray of snowman-shaped cookies out of the cooler and tie up a piping bag with blue frosting inside. But I haven't seen Roman yet today and I can't help but sneak glances.

"What are you looking for?" Kaylee winks at me. "Someone tall, handsome, and brooding?"

I tear my stare away from the window and draw a blue frosting outline on a cookie. "Stop it before I tell my brother that you called someone else handsome." I laugh.

"Go on and play your cards as close to your chest as you want to, but I would have to be dead not to notice the fireworks going off between the two of you. Maybe you could see whether he's going to the Christmas party. If he is... Maybe you could go with him, you know... like a date." Kaylee raises an eyebrow at me.

I put down my bag of frosting. "That's impossible for two reasons. One because I'm not going to the Christmas party since I don't have a sitter or an ugly sweater. And two because I did find myself attracted to him which can only mean there is something wrong with him. I'm not known for being a great picker of men."

"Well my sister Hannah is watching my daughter and I'm sure she can watch McKenna too. The girls love to play together. I can come up with a sweater for you, that's simple. And even if there's something wrong with Roman, he could be good for a night." Kaylee winks at me and I blush.

I abandon my mission of decorating the snowman cookies and step around the counter to sit with the kitties. "I can't argue with that. But we both know that's the last thing I need. I won't be bringing anyone into my world for a very long while. I'm going to commit my life and time to my daughter."

"The poor girl," Kaylee laughs. "McKenna wants a mom, not a best friend. You deserve to be happy too."

Kaylee was a single mother to her daughter Rosie until recently when she met and moved in with my brother Shawn. So if anyone is qualified to give me advice in this area, it's her.

"True as that may be, the only man I can trust right now is my brother. And even he has been cutting his eyes at my decisions lately. Looking over my shoulder. Second-guessing me." I shake my head. "You've got to tell him to take it down a notch."

"I know. I'm trying, but he worries too much. You'll find the right guy for you. He might be here sooner than we think."

Chapter Three: Roman

I normally don't make adjustments to my routine at work. Sticking to my schedule helps me stay grounded. But a week and a half after my initial visit to the cat cafe, stopping in has become a welcome addition to my daily routine.

I know that Stella isn't mine to take care of, but I like to check in anyway. Today I pull open the frosty door to the cat cafe just in time to see the chaos unfold.

Carole Cat leaps up from a hunkered position and attaches herself to the very top of the Christmas tree. With all the improvements I've made around here, making the Christmas tree catproof isn't something I've checked off my list.

The Douglas Fir bends like a palm tree in the wind and immediately I regret not making the time. I reach into the tree and hold it steady.

"Yay! You're here, I have something for you." Stella steps out from behind the counter. "This is a Christmas blend. I think you'll like it. It's practically holiday cheer in a mug." She hands me a warm cup of coffee.

I take it with one hand and use the other to keep the tree upright. "Thank you. I think Carole is trying to get herself on the naughty list up there."

"That is her favorite pastime. Now that I've buttered you up with a coffee, can I ask a big favor that you can totally say no to?" Stella scrunches her nose in the middle and I already doubt my ability to say no to her.

I let out a chuckle. "This is getting interesting."

"My daughter, McKenna, has a playhouse which is actually just an enormous box of parts right now. Can I hire you to come by and put it together sometime before Christmas?" She bites her bottom lip.

"Hire me? No. Absolutely not. But I'm happy to help in exchange for this coffee."

"Oh, thank you! It's a lot more work than I thought it would be when her dad dropped it off. He didn't exactly stick around to build it. So I opened it thinking it'd be a quick project and my eyes just about bugged out of my head." Stella raises onto her tiptoes and I can't help but notice the way her tits bounce under her apron.

"I was raised by a single mom. There isn't a higher calling. I'd be happy to stop by before Christmas and get it all set up." I like the idea of being a person Stella can depend on.

"It isn't so bad. In the beginning, I was terrified to be a single parent, but I'm settling into it."

"I've met your daughter, it seems like you're doing one hell of a job," I say.

Stella's face flushes pink and she runs a hand down my arm. Her touch shoots tingles through me and for a split second, I forget why my hand is buried in a tree.

The moment I let go, Carole Cat manages to send the whole Douglas Fir toppling to the ground. A cascade of red and gold Christmas balls bounce across the tile floor. The other two foster cats jump, frantically scurrying out of sight.

"Whoa, easy there Carole Cat, you've only got nine lives, eight now. That definitely cost you one." When I reach down to pick her up, Carole Cat lunges at me. She attaches herself to my chest, knocking me off balance.

I take a step back, white cat affixed to my snow jacket, and bump into Stella. In an attempt to shift my weight away from her, I throw my body in the other direction.

Stella reaches out to catch me like I don't outweigh her. Like she would be able to keep me on my feet. In the end, Carole Cat makes a run for it and I end up on my back. Stella lands firmly on top of me.

Her massive tits smash into my face and I decide that this is the luckiest day of my life. She smells like warm cinnamon and I try not to be a creep about the fact that her body fits mine like the missing piece to a puzzle.

Stella lets out a yelp and tries to scurry to her feet. But she isn't successful. Instead, she falls back on me, leaving us both red-faced and giggling out of control.

I lift my chin. "Well played Carole Cat. You'll see, I'm going to cat-proof that base. When I'm done, you'll be able to do pull-ups off that thing and it won't budge."

Then I look at Stella. With her mouth an inch from mine and our hearts beating in perfect rhythm, I'm taken aback. For a moment, I wonder what her lips would feel like pressed up against mine. I brush a strand of hair away from her face.

Ding.

"What the hell is this?" A man's voice booms as he steps inside.

"Shawn," Stella hops to her feet and I follow suit. She smoothes her apron. "Roman, this is my brother Shawn. Roman was helping me save the tree from falling at the paws of Carole Cat. Unsuccessfully, obviously."

"Nice to meet you." Shawn shakes my hand and his eyes lock onto mine. "I wasn't sure what I was looking at... caught me off guard."

"Roman's going to come by my house and build McKenna's playhouse for me," Stella says.

"He's stopping by your house..." Shawn looks at his sister in surprise.

"What can I say? Cute kid, cute mom, I didn't stand a chance." I chuckle, but Shawn doesn't follow suit.

Instead, his head turns back to me on a swivel. "You've met my niece?"

"When she was here the other day, yes." Stella shakes her head.

"Can I talk to you?" Shawn blinks deliberately at his sister and his tone is riddled with skepticism.

Smart man. If I were him I wouldn't want me anywhere near his sister or niece either. But Stella doesn't seem to catch on. She dismisses him with a casual wave of her hand.

"No. It's nice to see you here... at my work. Kaylee's in the back and she's waiting for you. Don't mess it up with her by wasting your time out here getting all weird right now." Stella ushers him toward the kitchen.

But Shawn hesitates, looking back and forth from his sister to me. "You know I could've just built it for you."

"Since when are you a carpenter? I want this thing to actually stand, you know, the doors to open." Stella laughs. "Are you going to keep your girlfriend waiting in there?"

With that Shawn turns his head. "Nice to meet you," he practically mumbles as he tears in through the door.

When he disappears, Stella turns to me. "Sorry about that, my brother has been a tad on the overprotective side since my divorce. He lost someone important to him once, so I don't hold his paranoia against him. But he can be annoying."

"That's what brothers are for and he doesn't have anything to worry about. I'm here to help because that's my job." I say it aloud more for myself than for her. I can't lose sight of the fact that I am not the kind of man someone like Stella should be dating. "Besides, I understand. You don't move on from a loss like that."

"Yeah. I just wish he trusted me to manage my own life. I'm not some sad fragile person longing for the past. I'm only embarrassed that I didn't get out of my relationship sooner." She smoothes her hair. "What about you? Are you in a relationship?"

"No, I'm not," I say simply. But when I notice the way my response makes her mouth turn up ever so slightly at the corner, I add. "And I can't be. They aren't for me. But I promise I'll get your daughter's playhouse up and running before Christmas. In the meantime, if you need anything here, I'm your man."

"Thank you. I appreciate that." Her mouth presses into a tight line.

I wonder if she's disappointed in my response or if I'm only imagining it. The truth is, I don't deserve to be happy and I most definitely don't deserve someone like Stella.

Shawn leaves and I keep my word by spending another two hours putting the Christmas tree back together. I create a cat-proof stand and wish Carole Cat good luck in trying to knock it down now. All the while, Stella keeps her distance.

When I finish, I head into the back and find Stella hard at work placing an order on the computer.

"Hey, I'm going to head out then. Carole's going to need a new hobby because she doesn't stand a chance at bringing that thing down now," I smile.

"She'll be so disappointed." Stella gives me a sweet smile. "Before you leave, I made this for you. It's just a thank you for all you've been doing around here." Stella slides an elaborately decorated sugar cookie across the counter to me.

"That's sweet of you. Thanks." The gesture warms me from the inside out.

"You're welcome, but you have to actually eat it. Don't just keep it because it's pretty to look at, then you'll miss the whole point," she says.

"Will do."

As I make my way out into the snow and toward the pub on the property, I tell myself to steer clear of Stella and the cafe for the next few days. I don't want to give her the wrong impression and I want to stay in control of my emotions. The more time I spend with her, the harder it gets.

Because what Stella can't possibly know with all her wide-eyed hopefulness is that the more I let her in, the more disappointed she'll be in the man I am.

My life is lonely. But if she could put loneliness next to the things I'm responsible for, she'd see that loneliness is a grace I've been given.

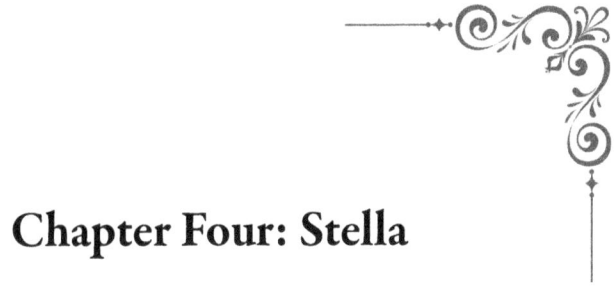

Chapter Four: Stella

Settling in with the girls for a night of gingerbread house crafting is just what I needed. Having Kaylee and her sister Hannah gathered around my kitchen table while Rosie and McKenna play together warms my heart. It's just the break I need from the monotony of my own thoughts.

"Do you have a glue gun? The carrot nose will not stay on my snowman and I think I'm past sticking these together with frosting." Hannah shoves an orange sprinkle into a dollop of white frosting. "They should give you enough to make it stick. Who makes a gingerbread house without a snowman out front?"

"I mean... lots of people," Kaylee laughs at her sister's lack of culinary skills.

Hannah and Kaylee banter back and forth and I get lost in my thoughts about Roman. Our last interaction was two days ago. One minute he's flirting with me, literally falling all over me, and the next he wants to make sure I know he can't or won't be in a relationship.

Then, he disappears. I haven't seen him since. I don't know if I'm being overly sensitive or if something is up with him. But an even better question is... *why do I care?*

I don't want to be in a relationship either. Has it been fun to flirt with Roman and get to know him? Yes. Have I had a few long nights fantasizing about him? Also yes. But that doesn't mean there's anything more between us.

I stick a row of white snowflake sprinkles to the roof of my gingerbread house. But when the room falls into a distinct hush, it snaps me back to the present. I look up, to find Kaylee and Hannah's eyes trained on me.

"What?" I ask.

"Nothing, you seem a little distracted is all," Kaylee says.

"You've been sticking the same row of sprinkles to the roof for ten minutes," Hannah bites back a giggle. "We have a question for you."

The sisters glance at each other. "Hannah wants to be your nanny!" Kaylee waves her fingers in the air.

"What? Would you be willing to do that? I know you already watch Rosie. Wouldn't it be too much?" The permanent tightness in my chest loosens just a bit.

"I would love to do it and I don't cancel on people." Hannah takes a sip of her tea and I fight the urge to lunge across the table and hug her.

"That's such a relief. Thank you." I didn't realize how stressed I've been about childcare until I notice I can breathe deeper all of a sudden.

"But I do have a condition... I hear there's a Christmas party you're avoiding. I'm watching the girls so you can go." Hannah shoots a look at her sister.

"And, I already got you a terrible, hideous, Christmas sweater to wear," Kaylee adds.

I shake my head with a chuckle. "Of all the things my brother has done for me in my life, and there have been many, bringing you two into it is the absolute top of the list."

"Ah, we are going to have so much fun!" Kaylee squeezes my forearm.

"So are we." Hannah smiles and gestures to McKenna and Rosie who are coloring together at the coffee table.

Our gingerbread houses take shape and I realize that I'm going to my first party for adults in a very long time. Now that I know McKenna will be taken care of, I feel a little buzz of nervous excitement at the idea.

Most people I work with either know me as Spencer's scorned ex-wife, or they don't know me at all. This is my chance to change that.

Creak.

When my front door pushes open, my brother Shawn steps inside without a thought of knocking, no doubt. It's another little quirk he's developed since my divorce.

"Uncle Shawn!" McKenna hops to her feet and rushes to him, throwing her arms around his legs and Rosie follows suit.

"Wow if it isn't my favorite ladies. What are we up to here?" Shawn asks.

"Coloring!" The girls take turns showing off their art and then bounce back to the coffee table.

Shawn comes into the kitchen and plants a kiss on the top of Kaylee's head. Watching the two of them fall in love has been so inspiring.

"Hi honey, we're just confirming that your sister here is heading to the Christmas party at work with us." Kaylee pats his hand as he rests it on her shoulder.

"Not with you. Alongside you. In my own car." I'll claim any bit of independence I can when it comes to my brother right now.

"Cool. Yeah. I meant to ask... who was that guy the other day at the cafe? Roman was it? Roman Stony." Shawn's casual tone isn't fooling me.

"Why do you know his last name? He's one of the Brewer property managers like he told you." I shake my head and thumb through my container of sprinkles.

"And..." Shawn raises an eyebrow at me expectantly swirling his wrist in my direction.

"And nothing, he's just a property manager." My face flushes red with heat.

"A property manager who has taken a special interest in you and my niece?" Shawn pushes the issue.

"I've heard he's something to look at but come on now, what's with the interrogation?" Hannah chimes in.

"Thank you," I say.

"I can't ask? I can't inquire as to what's happening in my sister's life?" Shawn feigns innocence and pulls up a chair.

"If you sit, I'm making you decorate a gingerbread house," I say.

"I'm going to be terrible at that," he lets out a laugh. "But, okay."

"Why don't you help with mine?" Kaylee inches toward him ever so slightly.

"Why don't I just admire you while you decorate?" Shawn wraps his arms around Kaylee.

Hannah rolls her eyes with a smirk in my direction. "Pass the blue sprinkles please."

"Here you go." Shawn slides the jar of sprinkles to Hannah. Then he turns his attention to me. "But seriously, what's the deal with this Roman guy? I got a weird feeling about him."

"We didn't even make it five minutes and you're already turning your attention back to my non-existent love life? Stop it. We all know I make bad choices when it comes to men. As paranoid as it's made you, just imagine what it's done to me. I'm making a point of enjoying my solitude after dealing with Spencer for so many years and I'm not looking to end this bliss anytime soon." I bite back a laugh and add, "When I do, I'm thinking you may have to be the last to know."

That's the truth. Or at least most of it. The rest of the truth is that it is nearly impossible for me to trust men right now no matter how charming or good-looking Roman might be.

"Fine, I get it. I'll back off. Forgive me for trying to take care of the world's cutest niece." Shawn heads into the living room and sits down between Rosie and McKenna.

Chapter Five: Roman

On the night of the office Christmas party, the Brewer brothers mob through their pub like a pack of wolves. If I walked beside them, I could probably blend in, but as friendly as they are, their bubble is impenetrable.

We might look similar, but our lives couldn't be more different. For starters, there are so many of them. They run a business together. They lean on each other. I imagine they never worry about whether they'll be alone on Christmas. I don't know how that feels.

I have friends, of course. Most of them are people I've met since I started working here at Brew by Brewer. The closest being my buddy Colt. He and I will get together for a few beers over the holiday.

Casual holidays with friends are all I know. Still, I imagine, it's not the same as what other people experience. So when the office holiday party comes around, I go. Even though it's a lot of people. Even though it's not really my thing. These people are the closest thing I have to an extended family, so I show up.

Even with all my willingness to bend my normal boundaries and participate, this year is pushing my limit. I have been asked to help by playing Santa since our hired Santa didn't show up.

I look like an idiot.

Thankfully, Stella isn't anywhere to be seen. So at the very least, I'm being spared the humiliation of wearing a fuzzy red suit in front of the most gorgeous woman in the world.

"Santa." Colleen from accounting is so close to my face it makes me shove my head back into the red velvet chair. She's swaying off-rhythm to the jazzy Christmas tune and holding a green Jello shot in her hand.

"Merry Chris..." I start but Coleen's alcohol-laden breath is enough to make me want to fall over. She paws at my chest and the gesture makes my skin crawl. "Never mind, you're done. Go ahead and step down before you fall."

"Aww, come on, you're supposed to be Santa, not the Grinch." She laughs but I don't join in.

Colleen is about the tenth sloppy drunk girl to throw herself at me tonight and we're only an hour into this party. When she takes it a step further and tries to straddle me, I get to my feet.

I adjust my fuzzy red Santa hat. "Excuse me." I push past her and head toward the bar.

"Santa," Colleen calls after me. She saunters past me wearing only a knitted vest and red shorts. When I don't stop, she keeps walking, making her way out onto the dancefloor and spinning around like a drunken mess.

I grab a bottle of water from behind the bar and glance at the clock. *How much longer am I going to be living this nightmare? In another half hour, I could probably slip out of the backdoor undetected. Why didn't Stella come? Why can't I stop thinking about her?*

The feel of a hand on my shoulder startles me back to the present. For a moment, I hope beyond reason that it might be Stella. But I step back in surprise when I turn and see that it's only her brother Shawn.

"Hey, Shawn Willman. Stella's brother we met the other day out at the cafe." He holds out his hand to me and when I shake it, Shawn holds firm for just a half-second too long.

"Hey man. You don't work here do you?"

"Nope. But my sister and my girlfriend do. Great party right? Like the outfit." Shawn orders a beer and tries for casual, but he misses the mark.

My mouth pulls sideways into a smirk. "Yeah. Thanks."

What's his angle?

"So how do you know the Brewers?" Shawn asks.

"How would I not know them? I work here and even though I didn't grow up in this town, it doesn't take long to run into at least one of them." I cut my eyes at him.

"Uh-huh. Cool. And before this?" Shawn's tone is breezy, but his eyes are fixed on mine.

Stella's brother approaching me is not exactly what I expected today. But I guess if Stella was my sister, I'd be looking out for her too. Especially with a guy like me hanging around. So I humor him by answering his question.

"Before this, I lived two hours from here in the big city my whole life. But I've been here for ten years and I've been at Brew by Brewer since they opened their doors. Other than that, I'm a fairly private person."

"Yeah, I—" He starts, but I cut him off.

"I need to head back to my uh, sleigh. See you around." I grab my water and step away from Shawn.

The truth is I can't blame the guy for wanting to keep his sister safe and away from me. I want that too. But I'm not about to let some dude dig into my past right here in the middle of an office Christmas party for a company he doesn't even work for.

I settle back into my sleigh. I tap my foot. I fidget in my seat. I'm more unsettled than I'd like to admit about Shawn's inquiries.

When I glance across the room to look at the clock, I see Stella and my heart skips a beat. She's stunning, even in an ill-fitting, knitted, sweater with a cat and Christmas tree on the front.

She carries herself with such poise and grace. That's the thing about Stella, she's so opposite of me in every way. My whole life, I've had this thing where I repel people. But she's like a magnet. Even though she isn't trying, she turns heads.

I watch her as she makes her way through the room with Kaylee by her side. Leaving each person she talks to with a smile. The way she looks around the room makes me think she's looking for someone and I wonder irrationally if that person could be me.

Another five minutes is all it takes to decide that hanging back is just plain rude. Even if I keep falling hard for Stella, I don't have to actually date her. I can be her friend, keep her safe until her equal comes along. That would be enough for me... Probably.

I stand to go find her but as I do, Brandon Brewer takes the microphone at the front of the room. The first item on his laundry list of announcements is the opportunity to take a photo with Santa.

Dammit.

As soon as the Christmas music comes back on, a group of women approaches me, cellphones in hand. I know I'm trapped, at least for now. So I sit back down and smile through gritted teeth as I lose sight of Stella in the crowd.

Chapter Six: Stella

I'm so happy Hannah and Kaylee convinced me to come to this party in this ridiculous sweater. My hair is done up with red and green ribbons and handmade Christmas bulb earrings finish the look.

There's a novelty to being here without my child. My only goal is to have the best night ever. I forgot how much fun it is to chat with other adults. By large, the people who work at Brew by Brewer are genuinely kind.

I will admit that I'm disappointed not to have run into Roman, but I suppose these things aren't for everyone. Still, I'm having a great time. I promised McKenna I'd take a picture with Santa, so that's next on my list. When it's finally my turn, I take a step forward onto the platform.

When Santa lifts his gaze to mine, it is instant fireworks. I'd recognize Roman's smoldering eyes anywhere. Seeing them peeking out between a white beard and a fuzzy red hat makes my heart leap in my chest.

"Roman, are you Santa? Is that where you've been the last few days? At the North Pole, making toys?" My voice is a low whisper and I can't help the giggle that escapes my lips.

"My secrets out." Roman throws his head back and lets out a chuckle. "No, I was just giving you space."

"Who said I needed space?" I tuck a strand of hair behind my ear and watch as a flash of something crosses Roman's face, though I can't say what it is for sure, it looks a little like longing. "When you said you'd do anything the Brewers needed you to, you weren't kidding. I like that in a man."

"Well, I like a beautiful woman in a cat sweater. So I guess we're both in luck today. Are you gonna get in here and get your picture?" Roman spreads his legs and holds his arms out to me.

I lean gently onto his knee, but Roman wraps his hands around my waist and pulls me back into him. I revel in the heat that radiates between us. Leaning back into the comfort of his broad chest, I grin as the photographer snaps away.

"Hey everyone, hope your night is off to a great start." Brandon Brewer taps the microphone, interrupting our photoshoot, and the room falls silent.

I make no attempt to get off Roman's lap and he doesn't seem to mind. He pulls me in even closer and nuzzles into the back of my neck. The heat of his breath on my skin makes goosebumps ripple across me.

Brandon continues, "I'd like to invite everyone to meet us just through the doors behind you for the three-legged candy cane race. Here are the rules. Grab your partner and tie up your legs. You each need to hold your candy cane with one finger. If your candy cane falls or if you touch it with more than one finger, you lose. The winner gets New Year's Eve off. Let's do this."

A mass of people wander out into the enormous back room attached to the pub. It's stunning with its vaulted ceilings and white Christmas lights overhead. A picture-perfect winter wonderland.

"What do you say Santa, can you be my partner?" I get to my feet.

"I think I can." Roman stands and puts a hand on my lower back, steering me off the Santa platform.

"You know what? Let's stop by the bar first. I see a red, gingerbread martini with my name on it."

"I don't drink actually. Alcoholism runs in my family, my mom and brother too. It isn't something I mess with. But you most definitely deserve to have one or two... or five. Whatever you want. I'm here to make sure nothing bad happens to you. Enjoy your night, I've got you covered. I can drive you home if need be."

"Thank you, that's really sweet." And a huge change. I all but stopped drinking while I was with Spencer knowing that there was a good chance I'd have to be responsible for getting us both home safely.

I order my drink and I can't ignore the way Roman's eyes glide across me. His stare, lingering on my lips.

"So what are your plans for Christmas? Probably the whole Santa thing."

"Yes, my brother Shawn and his girlfriend Kaylee are hosting this year. It'll be a classic Willman family affair with all the trimmings. Eggnog, board games, you know, the works. What about you?"

"I don't have a family but I get together with my buddy Colt. Maybe you know him? He runs the golf course here." Roman reaches for his wallet and pays for my drink without missing a beat.

"Thank you, you didn't have to do that. I don't think I've met Colt yet, but is he here ton—" I stop talking when I notice Shawn lurking in the corner, watching us like a total weirdo.

I shake my head and Roman follows my line of sight.

"It's my brother. I'm sorry. I think he's more upset about my last relationship than I am. He's not normally this crazy, he's actually a pretty reasonable guy."

Roman waves off my apology. "Don't worry about it. He's just looking out for you. Come on, let's get into that competition."

Ten minutes later, Roman and I are tied up together, though not in the way I'd like. But this is better than nothing. For now, I relish the feeling of his side bound to mine.

Roman drapes an arm over my shoulder. "We've got this."

"Yeah, we do." I lean into him.

"Or maybe *we* do." Shawn's voice sounds from behind us. I let out a laugh when Kaylee mouths the words, *I'm sorry,* in my direction.

I look up at Roman, an apologetic smile resting on my lips.

"Don't worry, I have a plan." Roman winks at me.

When the whistle blows, Roman tosses his candy cane to the ground. He wraps his arms around my waist and lifts me up. He takes off in a full sprint in the opposite direction from the finish line.

I laugh until tears are pouring down my face as he bounces us straight out of the crowd and back into the now vacant pub. When we're alone tucked into a back corner, he puts me down.

"See, I won. Now I get you here all to myself." Roman pulls me in close to him.

When his mouth lands on mine it takes my breath away. His pillow-soft touch sends sparks of electricity wafting over me. He uses his tongue to part my lips. Roman holds me so tight I swear I can feel his heartbeat in my own chest. Our breathing syncs and I am weak in the knees.

I wish I could stay here like this with him forever lost in the promise of what could be between us. As irresponsible as it is I want to give myself to Roman in every way.

But I don't care because tonight I don't feel like a mom. Tonight I feel like myself for the first time in a long time. That's a gift Roman has given me. I missed the girl I used to be, and now that she's back, I think it's only fair I give her what she wants.

I hear the rumblings of the masses heading back toward us. Without giving it another thought I lean in toward Roman. The swell of my chest pressing against him. I drop my voice to a whisper. "Get me out of here."

At first I'm not sure if he hears me because he doesn't do anything, he just stands there holding me. His hand is in my hair, his heart pounding in his chest. I run my hand on the back of his neck and tilt his head down to mine.

When our eyes meet, I say it again with conviction. "Roman, I want you to get me out of here and get my clothes off."

This time there isn't any question as to whether or not he heard me. Roman interlaces my fingers with his and in an instant, he's tossing my snow jacket at me. Then we're running across the snowy bank to the hotel like two kids trying to sneak out without being caught.

Roman pulls keys out of his pocket and unlocks a back door. We slip inside and I push close to him as the warm air penetrates my jacket. Roman leads us up a back staircase and down the hotel's long hallway. When he stops in front of the last hotel room on the right, I look up at him.

"Do you have a room here tonight?" I ask.

Roman looks at me, his mouth curled into a smile on one side. "Sweetheart, I have the key to every room here, every night."

I look into his eyes and I know without a doubt that nothing will ever be the same.

Chapter Seven: Roman

I t's been a long while for me. Too long. I struggle to maintain control of myself as I wrestle Stella's clothes off of her. But it helps that she seems just as eager as I am, ripping the shapeless sweater off her body and tossing it onto the floor. Within seconds the Santa suit follows.

Stella throws herself back onto the bed, splaying herself out and making my mouth water. Her tits are a perfect handful, bouncing with her movement and creating a sight I'll never forget.

"You're gorgeous." My heart pounds in my chest. "It's like the best Christmas present ever."

Stella lets out a giggle. Then she hooks my arm with hers and tugs me forward, kissing the breath out of me. "Why don't you finish unwrapping your gift?"

From there it's a blur, a frenzied rush of heat crackling through me. I'm running my hands over her stomach and across her hips. I'm grabbing her tits and pinching her nipples between my fingers. I'm devouring every curve and reveling in the sensation of her skin against mine.

Stella spreads her legs and slips two fingers inside, stretching herself open for me. Her glistening wet slit makes my mouth water and there's already tension working through my spine.

I slide a hand down and squeeze my pulsating length. I can't help myself. She drives me wild as she bucks and thrusts her hips until I replace her hand with my own.

"No, I don't want your fingers. Get your cock in me." Stella's words come out in a rush of breath that sends tingles across my body.

It's the kind of order you just can't refuse.

I shift forward, planting myself between her legs. I roll my hips toward her, my tip beading with lust. I start my push inside and get halfway in before I have to pause to let her catch her breath. She's tight and I'm so wound up I don't want to hurt her.

But Stella nods for me to continue, spreading her legs even wider and taking in my sizable girth. When I push all the way inside, she throws her head back and lets out a long, toe-curling, moan.

Once I'm inside of her, I hold her there, savoring the moment. Stella's face flushes with the prettiest shade of red. The blush extends down the sides of her neck and tapers at the swell of her cleavage.

But it doesn't take long for Stella to make it clear that slow isn't what she's looking for. Her nails leave brilliant red stinging welts on my ass and the curve of my back. She lets out a whimpering moan for more.

I bend down and run my tongue over the curve of her breast, slipping a nipple between my lips. I pull two sharp sucks before her hands are digging at my backside, pushing me into moving faster, harder, deeper. It's another offer I'm not going to refuse.

I rock into Stella and her walls are tight and slick around me. She makes me tingle and throb. It's unfathomable that someone like me should be able to hold someone like Stella so close. That somehow, even with all that's gone wrong in my life, I should get to be here with the sexiest woman I've ever met.

My body jumps and jerks as I struggle to keep my cool. I'm eager for more of her. Desperate. Hungry. I slam myself into her so hard it makes the headboard rattle against the wall behind us.

After that, I'm insatiable. I lean forward, bracing my forehead against her shoulders. My hands dig into her hips so tight I worry I'm going to leave bruises.

Stella shifts, reaching down and pushing her fingers against the spot where we're joined together. As we move in tandem, she strokes my length and it's pure ecstasy.

The sound of my name on her lips spurs me on. I wrap a fistful of her hair around my hand and tug exposing her neck. Then I clench my teeth and press my mouth against her. When I bite down, it gets me a gasp and a moan of pleasure from her pretty mouth. So I do it a second time, only harder.

Stella's body stiffens. Her walls tighten and clench around me and I lose control. I pound into her again and again. Grunting. Grinding my hips. Thrusting deep before hammering her with short shallow thrusts that punch the breath right out of her.

Stella moans, chanting my name. Her breasts smack together. Tremors build in her body until she's shaking from head to toe. Finally, she explodes, collapsing along my length and covering me in slick streams.

Watching her come undone like that makes heat build low in me. A cum slick hand reaches down, grabbing and tugging at my balls. It's enough to push me over the edge.

I sink into the side of Stella's neck again and bite down hard. My own release rips through me like a bolt of lightning and Stella doesn't stop. She milks me to the last drop. I stay there, pulsating inside of her while I catch my breath.

Chapter Eight: Stella

An hour later, Santa and I stumble back into the party washed in the warm afterglow of the most amazing sex of my life. I'm helplessly giddy and dare I say, in love.

Roman buys me a red cocktail with sugar on the rim. And when I find myself standing under a sprig of mistletoe hanging from the ceiling, Roman wraps himself around me like a warm blanket on a cold night.

His kisses devour me and I let myself drown in him. I'm lost in his embrace. I feel taken care of. It's a new sensation for me. Roman pours himself over the top of me and growls sweet words in my ear that make me blush as I sip my cocktail.

Roman and I are tucked away into a back corner, his lips are on my neck. I could stay here forever with him, lost in our own little world.

"There you are. I need to talk to you right now." My brother's voice booms from over my shoulder, shattering my bliss bubble.

I can't help but roll my eyes. I love my brother but honestly, I'm a grown woman. If I want to make out with hot-Santa at a party, that's on me. Roman keeps his hand on my lower back as he looks past me to Shawn.

"Now, Stella. Come on." Shawn's nostrils flare and his eyebrows furrow together. He's red in the face.

"Are you insane? Relax Shawn, it's a party." I blink at him in total confusion.

Shawn wraps his hand around my wrist and tugs me toward him. "I need to talk to you outside."

I glance at the falling snow in the dark night and jerk my arm back. "We can talk but I'm not going out there. What's wrong with you? I'll be right back." I look at Roman with an apologetic smirk and a shrug.

Shawn turns in a snap and all but drags me away from Roman. When we get into the hall and out of earshot, Shawn pulls out his phone. "I know you're not going to like this and I'm sorry, but I did it anyway. You have to trust me when I tell you I was looking out for you and for McKenna. I hired a private investigator to look into Roman."

I blink up at my brother, not even sure how to react. One part of me is enraged and the other part only feels shock. My brother has always been protective of me. But since I've gotten divorced Shawn's intrusion into my life has gotten out of control.

My jaw clenches. "Are you kidding me? Shawn, I'm an adult. It's like you don't even trust me with my own daughter. I know that Spencer was not a good person. That wasn't a surprise. I was making the best of a bad situation so my kid could have her father in her life. But I'm not an idiot. I can make my own choices and you're going to have to trust that. You were wrong to hire someone, Roman is a good man."

"Listen, this isn't about being right. In fact, I hoped that I wouldn't find anything. If that was the case I would never have even told you."

"That doesn't make it any better! Not telling me is creepy, a total violation of my privacy..." My stomach swirls with nausea. "Wait. What do you mean *if* you didn't find anything?"

Shawn holds up his phone. "You're not going to like what he found. I'm sorry to have to be the one to tell you this, but Roman's brother is dead. Roman went to prison shortly after. He has some kind of sealed record that coincides with the dates."

"What?"

"You can read it all right here for yourself. It's going to take a little longer before we know exactly what it's about, but from what I can tell so far, it doesn't look good. I'm worried you aren't being safe. You're bringing him into your world so quickly... You let him meet McKenna."

"I didn't let him meet her. McKenna was there at work, Spencer didn't show up to take her... and my babysitter..." I can't even think over the sound of blood rushing to my ears.

McKenna is my daughter. I make the decisions for her, not Shawn... But what if he's right? What if my tendency to find the wrong guys is only getting worse with age?

"It's okay we just need—" He starts but when the door opens and Roman steps into the hall, Shawn stops talking.

"Everything okay out here?" Roman's smile fades quickly as his eyes dart back and forth between Shawn and me.

I freeze, swallowing the lump in my throat. My brain can't pair the information Shawn just dropped on me with the charming man standing in front of me. It can't be true. I feel like I might fall over.

Shawn steps forward, putting his body between Roman and me. "It's up to you how we move forward," my brother mumbles to me.

I inhale through my nose and collect myself before taking a step forward. My voice wobbles. "Roman, I'm only going to ask you once, did your being in prison have anything to do with your brother's death?"

The words hang in the silent space between us, sucking up all the air in the hall. I watch in horror as the color drains from Roman's face.

Roman's lips part and then purse back together. The muscles in his throat clench and his shoulders slump forward ever so slightly. He takes in a deep breath through his nose and on the exhale, he gives the one-word answer that changes everything.

"Yes."

Chapter Nine: Roman

"Yes." I don't know how else to answer Stella's question but with the simplest version of the truth.

I feel dizzy and sick to my stomach. I don't know where that question came from or how he got his information. I don't know why Shawn felt so entitled to talk about the absolute worst years of my life in the middle of a Christmas party.

But as the room spins around me, I understand this... the *why* doesn't matter at this point. The damage is done. I can see it all over Stella's blank face.

I'm overwhelmed with emotion and honestly shocked. The situation was complex and traumatic and it's one I try not to think about often. Still, it's never far from my mind.

There's of course more to the story, but details aren't what Stella asked for. Besides, in a room of drunken co-workers, it's hardly the time. Not to mention the fact that Shawn has positioned himself between Stella and me as if I would ever hurt her. As if he could stop me if I did want to. What a joke.

I keep my face still as my heart rate ticks up and sweat beads on my back. When I take a step toward her, Stella's body stiffens. Then she takes one massive, heartbreaking step away from me.

Her eyes round and water pools in the corners. This is a look that I can only imagine equates to something like, pure terror. But Stella is seeing me for the broken man I am and I suppose it's only fair.

"Hey, listen..." I reach out my hand for her forearm but Shawn pushes me away.

"Watch it," Shawn glares at me.

"I just want to talk—" I start.

"Roman I need to go," Stella calls out to me from behind her brother's massive-too-big shoulders.

I take a step back and shove my hands in my pockets. "Okay," is all I manage to get out.

There isn't any point in explaining myself. In fact, it's probably better this way. The truth is, if I let her in she'd only be disappointed in the end anyway.

As they walk away, Stella's brother Shawn looks over his shoulder. He cuts his eyes at me and curls his mouth into one final look of pure disdain. I can't blame him. His sister is something special and I am completely undeserving of her. We both know it.

Stella and I were never going to happen, at least not in the long run. I don't know what kind of fantasy world I let myself get lost in. But guys like me don't end up with women like Stella.

Stella is a beautiful woman from an upper-middle-class background. She's a mother. She's smart, funny, and independent. Stella would make any man the happiest man on earth.

And I don't deserve to be happy. With what I've done, sitting in jail was the least I could do. What I deserve is to switch places with my brother.

The worst part is that truth be told, I might make the same choices all over again if I found myself in that situation today. I have no way of knowing because I lost control of myself at that moment.

The dark shadows that took up residence in my mind for so many years creep back into the corners. I'm headed back to cold, dark, and lonely. I can feel it.

A single question erased the bright light of hope that Stella brought into my world. I'm back to being me... a sinner who will spend a lifetime repenting. I step back inside and the room seems to spin around me and my throat runs dry.

"Hey Santa, why so sad? Want me to unwrap your package?" The slurred come-on hardly registers in my mind.

"I'll bet I can make you jolly," another random, slurred voice joins in the mix.

My feet cement themselves to the floor. I know in my heart of hearts that I just lost the best thing that's ever happened to me.

"Hey man, you alright?" My coworker Colt's voice rings loud in my ears puncturing my thoughts and I turn to face him.

"Fine. I'm fine."

"I think Santa has some fans over there ready to get some pictures taken," he chuckles.

"Yeah." I focus on putting one foot in front of the other, getting to my sleigh, and then falling into it. An hour passes in a blur of drunken coworkers plopping themselves onto my lap. I keep an eye on Shawn. He seems to do the same for me. But his sister isn't anywhere to be found.

I stay frozen, finishing out my commitment for the night. A smirk rests permanently on my lips because I'm not able to work up to a full smile. Not now. My body is here but my mind is with Stella.

The way she gave herself to me rocked my world. The sex was incredible. Mind-blowing. But now, none of that matters because she's probably at home disgusted that she let herself get entangled with a monster like me.

"Hey, how are you holding up?" Colt's voice breaks through my thoughts. "You aren't looking so hot, maybe you should call it a night."

"I said I would be here, so I'm waiting out the hour." I wipe my sweaty palms on the top of my red pants.

"I mean it dude, come on." Colt gestures for me to join him and I follow.

When we get to the bar he hands me a glass of water. I put a hand to the back of my neck and roll my head around, trying to loosen the tight muscles.

"Thanks. Yeah, I'm not feeling well."

"I can tell. One too many drunk accountants falling all over you?" Colt chuckles.

"Something like that."

"Head home, it's just a few minutes until you're done anyway, right? I'm heading over to chat with Brandon right now, I'll let him know." Colt claps me on the back with a laugh. "Get some sleep, you look like shit bro."

"Thanks for that one," I snort out a chuckle.

I look at Colt as he turns to chat with Brandon Brewer. Colt is a good dude. An ex-professional golfer who runs the course out at Brew by Brewer. Young. Thoughtful. He comes from money and a good family, but he's chill about it.

He's the kind of uncomplicated guy Stella deserves. The kind of man McKenna could look up to. I take a step toward the exit then stop in my tracks.

McKenna.

My heart thuds in my chest. *The playhouse. Shit.*

I think back to the look on McKenna's face the day she sat with me on the porch of the cafe. She asked about her playhouse. Then I made a promise to Stella that I would get it done for her before Christmas.

Stella will move on, I know that. I don't need to clear my name with her or make her listen to a long-drawn-out sob story. But I do want to keep my promise. Standing behind my word is all I have and I don't want to let that go. I turn on a dime. I know exactly where I need to start.

It isn't hard to find Shawn in the crowd, mostly because he's still turning to stare at me every few minutes. Now he's standing beside the Christmas tree and it seems like as good a time as any.

I can't blame the guy for being protective of his sister but I hope he's willing to hear me out. I make eye contact and approach him with slow caution.

"Hey man, I just want to talk." I hold my hands up.

Shawn's mouth turns down at the corners. "This should be good." He crosses his arms over his chest.

"I'll leave her alone. I get it. But there's one thing I need to do first and I'm going to need your help."

Shawn pauses. The tight lines that crease his forehead soften and he excuses himself from the group he's standing with. I follow him to the back of the room and he turns to me.

"My sister seems to like you, so I'm listening. But I'm telling you right now, after what I've watched her go through with her jackass of an ex-husband, I'm not in the mood to entertain any kind of bullshit. She's a good person. A mom. She deserves a decent guy in her life." Shawn gives me a nod.

"I get that and I agree with you. Everything you saw in that report is true. If you give me the chance, I'll tell you exactly what will come back when they unseal the details. It isn't a part of my life I'm proud of but I own it."

From there Shawn isn't necessarily kind but to his credit the man is fair. He hears me out. He lets me tell the entire story from top to bottom. As painful as it is, I don't leave out any details.

When I get to the gut-wrenching part of the story where I have to tell Shawn that I lost my brother to alcohol, his face softens and his arms fall to his sides.

In an instant, I go from thinking he might punch me to wondering whether I should offer him a chair. But Shawn manages to stay on his feet. Then he shocks me by sharing a story of his own.

Shawn tells me that he too has suffered a significant loss in his life due to alcohol. His young son was killed in a car crash with a drunk driver behind the wheel.

As Shawn talks, I can see the pain radiating off his skin like a wave of heat. And just like that, we connect. In the middle of an office Christmas party, dressed in a Santa suit, I have one of the most meaningful conversations of my entire life. I decide that Shawn Willman is a quality person.

He's compassionate and flawed. He understands more about loss than he lets on, and he's been given a second chance at happiness in his life. On top of that, Shawn has an impressive understanding of the way his sister's mind works and he shares it with me.

In the end not only do I not mind the guy, but I like him. I'm grateful that Stella has a man like him in her life. A sense of peace washes over me.

I may not ever get to be the man in Stella and McKenna's lives, but I know they'll be taken care of with Shawn lurking around the corner. He'll be there, watching their every move like some kind of sibling vigilante.

Before we're done, I ask Shawn to help me keep my final promise to McKenna and Stella by helping me gain access to Stella's yard to build the playhouse. When he agrees, I feel the tightness in my chest ease just a bit.

"Can we do it while she's at work? I don't want to disturb her. She doesn't even need to know it was me, you can have all the credit on this one. And after getting her new boyfriend investigated behind her back, you may need it." I let out a humorless chuckle.

"I know that's right. Yeah, we'll work something out."

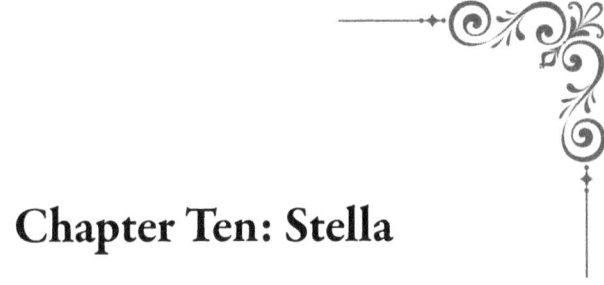

Chapter Ten: Stella

I make the decision to leave the party early, after all that's happened, what choice did I have? Could I really stay and dance the night away with jailhouse-Santa and my brother breathing down my neck?

I know my absolute devastation is irrational given the fact that Roman and I hardly know each other. But somehow, I thought I knew his heart. Even after all my mistakes in choosing the wrong men, I trusted my gut and it's led me right back here. Alone in my car making my way back to my daughter.

I grip my steering and let out a desperate, manic laugh in the solitude of the front seat of my car. My head whirls with the reality of the situation unfolding in front of me like a nightmare. My stomach turns and my thoughts jumble, but they boil down to just three main mantras that pound in my mind.

I am a mother. I should have known better. What kind of danger could I have been putting my daughter in?

I should have stuck to my original plan. After my failed wedding, I told myself to put my head down and worry only about McKenna from here on out. That would have been the safer option.

I should have hidden away somewhere for five, maybe ten years before I even considered dating again. But instead, I opened the door for heartbreak, chaos... and who knows what else?

I'm not crazy about the idea of Shawn going behind my back to investigate Roman. But in light of the findings, I can't possibly be mad at Shawn. As it turns out, my brother's hunch about Roman was right.

Yet even now with as dumb as I feel, I have to admit that there's a part of me that doesn't believe Roman could be a bad guy. He's sweet. Charming. Unassuming. And possibly the best actor in the world, I guess.

The details of Roman's situation are still blurry, but I don't know how much they matter. After all, Roman admitted that he ended up in jail with a sealed record after an event related to his brother's death.

By the time I pull into the driveway at Hannah's place, I'm emotionally exhausted. When I walk through the front door, I'm ready to grab my daughter and head home.

"Mom!" McKenna and Rosie pause their game long enough to smile at me.

"Hi, what are you two up to?" I start but by the time I get my question out, they are lost in chatter and fits of giggles. I'm happy to see that at least one of us is having a perfect night.

"Hey, you're back early. How was it?" Hannah asks.

"It was... interesting. Thanks so much for watching McKenna. How'd it go for you, being outnumbered by six-year-olds and all?"

"It was great, McKenna is always such a big help. It's actually easier to watch both of them together because they love to play and they never stop giggling." Hannah pauses and looks me up and down. "Why *are* you back so early and where are my sister and Shawn? Is everything okay?"

I pull out a chair and sit at her kitchen table. "It is and it isn't. I had such a good time at the party... with Roman."

Hannah's eyes widen and a smile tugs at the corner of her mouth. "Ah, okay I see... Did you two, you know?" She glances at the kids then drops her voice to a whisper. "Kiss?"

I bite my bottom lip and smile at the memory, giving her a nod. "More actually. But almost immediately after, I found out that Roman isn't exactly who I thought he was. I just let him into my heart, and my world without even knowing him. I feel like I let myself down and somehow, McKenna too."

Hannah looks over her shoulder at McKenna who is currently hosting a tea party. "I think she'll recover."

"Yeah, probably." I can't help but let out a chuckle.

"You sound like my sister right before she met Shawn. She was determined to raise Rosie on her own. But the most amazing thing happened. Your brother made Kaylee a happier, more trusting person and Rosie reaped all the benefits. I think you'd be surprised how much McKenna probably wants happiness for you. It's too bad Roman wasn't your person, but you should keep trying." Hannah pours me a cup of tea and slides it across the wood table.

"Thanks." I take a sip. "I just keep thinking about the example I'm setting for McKenna. I want her to grow up and choose a man who's going to stick around and take care of her in the long run. But more than that, I want her to know that she can do things on her own. I want her to be independent and I want those things for me too."

Hannah wrinkles her forehead. "It isn't one or the other. You don't have to trade your independence for a relationship, at least not when it's the right guy." She laughs. "I mean, who am I to say, I haven't met my right guy yet."

"Maybe he's out there hanging out with my right guy. They're looking for us, but we're hiding away in here with tea and kids," I laugh.

"If that's the case I wish they'd come on over already." Hannah finishes her tea. "But honestly, I think one of the best gifts you could give McKenna is a happy mom. It takes a strong person to put yourself out there knowing that there's a chance of being hurt in hopes of finding something real. McKenna's going to be okay in this life. She has Shawn and my sister. She has me and Rosie. More than that, she has the best mom. I don't think you need to worry about McKenna. I think the best thing you could do for McKenna is to take care of yourself."

"Ugh, it's so much easier to take care of other people." I take a sip of tea to hide my smile.

"So can I ask what Roman did that was so awful? Because he sounded amazing. Was he..." Hannah lowers her voice. "Bad in bed?"

"No, definitely not the problem. The truth is I don't know exactly what he did, but I know it wasn't good. I only know because Shawn hired someone behind my back to look into Roman. Apparently what the investigator found wasn't great. Roman had a brother who passed away and he spent some time in jail because of it."

"Wait a minute, this guy killed his brother?" Hannah's voice goes shrill and high-pitched.

"Shh, no! Of course not. Roman wouldn't be walking the Brew by Brewer property like he owns it if he did. But something happened, the investigation concluded that some of his records were sealed so we won't know until he does some more digging. Not that it matters at this point." A pit forms in my stomach just thinking about it.

"Wait, are you telling me you don't even know what the issue was? Forget about the investigator, what did Roman say when you asked him?" Hannah looks at me, her eyes flicking up and down, searching my face. Then her mouth falls open. "You didn't give him a chance to explain? You two didn't step away from that brother of yours and talk about it?"

My throat runs dry. "No, I guess we didn't."

"You're really upset about this. You're falling for him. That deserves a conversation."

I nod. "I haven't been in love for a very long time. But Roman rocked my world. He's chivalrous. The kind of guy that knows how to treat a woman... And maybe also a felon of some sort." I shrug.

Hannah raises an eyebrow. "I hate to bring up the obvious but don't you think you should ask him to explain what happened before you give up all your hopes, dreams, and good sex?" Hannah lowers her voice and I can't help but let out a giggle.

"Well if you're going to be logical about this I can't argue with you. I wasn't thinking, the whole thing caught me off guard."

Hannah leans across the table. "Okay listen, I need to hear the whole story, from the top..."

By the time I finish chit-chatting with Hannah, it's late. I drag McKenna home and she falls asleep before I make it into her room to say goodnight. As I cover her with a blanket and kiss her head, I think about Hannah's words.

The best thing you can give McKenna is a happy mom.

In my heart of hearts, I know Hannah is right. Until Roman came into my world, it had been a long time since I'd thought about what truly makes me happy.

With Spencer, it was always about him. Helping him. Fixing him. Building up his ego. Then even after McKenna surprised us by coming into the world before either of us were ready to be a parent, it somehow stayed all about Spencer. Helping him be a good dad. Making sure I didn't neglect him by becoming consumed with the baby.

The thing we fought about most wasn't the lies or the cheating. It was time. I lost myself in those years of desperately trying to keep my family intact. Now as I pack McKenna's bag for her first overnight stay at her dad's apartment, I can't help but see the irony in the situation. The minute she heads out of the door all I'll have is time.

Spencer remained consistently selfish throughout our relationship. I've learned that when people show you who they are you should believe them the first time. and that is a part of why I'm struggling with the news about Roman.

In the past few weeks, Roman has shown me who he is. Consistent. Sweet. Protective. Nothing he's done gives me any reason for concern.

When I lay down, my eyes are heavy but I can't get the thoughts of Roman out of my mind. The secrets uncovered by the investigator are totally out of left field. If it were just me, I think I might not even care to know. But it isn't only me. I have a little girl who trusts me to keep her safe and that thought weighs heavy on my heart.

WHEN I WAKE UP THE next morning, I do so knowing that I need to talk to Roman first thing. I owe it to both of us to hear him out. Between getting McKenna packed for her Dad's house and getting myself out to the cat cafe, I don't have time to make the call.

Instead, I spend the morning watching out of the big, picture windows of the cafe and hoping to see a figure crunching through the snow in the distance.

But Roman never comes and by the afternoon my heart is broken all over again.

"Have you talked to him?" Kaylee asks.

"No, and I'm not feeling very good about it. Plus, McKenna is at her dad's place overnight for the first time. It all just feels... bad."

"I've been there. It isn't fun. You should head home early. I've got this."

Chapter Eleven: Roman

With all the hustle Shawn and I have put into this project today, I still wasn't ready for Stella to come home. Shawn was under the impression that she'd be gone for a few more hours.

The last thing I wanted was to be standing in her backyard like some kind of stalker... but here we are.

Stella has flipped on the lights on her back patio and I'm caught. My brain scrambles, sifting through my options, but none of them are clear. My heart thuds in my chest. All I can think to do is stand here with my mouth hanging open like an idiot.

Stella on the other hand seems to know exactly how she wants to handle this situation. Her eyes widen and then narrow on me. She puts a hand on her hip and rips open her sliding glass door.

"What is this? What are you doing?" Her tone is as sharp as glass and her eyes roam across the smattering of tools scattered at my feet. "Now you're breaking into my backyard? This isn't okay, I have a child."

I hate the way her face is twisted into a panic. I hate it even more that I'm the one who caused her to look like that.

I hold my hands up. "Shawn was here with me all day."

"What are you talking about? You got my brother more involved than he already was?" Stella presses her fingers to her temples.

I thought telling her that Shawn was on board with my plan would be a comfort, but somehow I seem to have made things worse. *How am I messing this up so badly when all I'm trying to do is make things right?*

"Stella listen. Shawn knows everything. I told him the whole truth about everything in that report and I'll tell you too if you let me. Do you think he'd let me live if I was here as some kind of creep just wandering through your yard? Come on." I shake my head. "I wanted to do something nice. Keep my promise to you and then be on my way. I didn't expect you'd be back so soon."

She stays frozen.

I continue, "Call your brother and ask, he's on his way back now. He only went to the hardware store. If it makes you feel better, call him now, I mean it." I take a step backward. The absolute last thing I wanted to do was make Stella feel uncomfortable in her own home.

"I don't know what's happening here but I feel like I can't trust anything." Stella steps out onto the back patio, which is a good sign, I think. At least she isn't scared of me.

Stella sits with perfect posture on the metal outdoor chair and crosses her arms over her chest. I keep a cautious distance before pulling out a chair and joining her uninvited.

She looks at me. "What happened to your brother?" Her mouth hardly moves as she speaks.

Stella is the last person in the world I want to disappoint. But right now, I have no choice other than to take a deep inhale of breath through my nose and come clean.

"This is the whole truth. I never knew my father and my mother struggled with alcohol abuse. So I grew up taking care of my brother and I did the best I could. I should've done better. Tried harder. Paid more attention." The words burn as they leave my throat.

Stella's face softens and she leans in toward me ever so slightly.

"My mom passed along her addiction to my brother. Before either he or I could get a hold of it, the drinks took him over like a hurricane. I don't like starting his description like that because he wasn't just some addict. He was a person and he was trying. He wanted to get sober and change his life. He was so much more than his addiction." My throat tightens. Even after all this time, the hurt hasn't gone away. "The night that my brother died was my fault."

Stella's eyes soften, but her posture goes rigid and she pulls her hand off me. She leans back, keeping her distance. "Go on."

I blow out a heavy breath and my chest tightens. I clear my throat. "I knew he was down. Looking back, it was so obvious that he needed me. He had just been dumped, he was between jobs. My plan was to stay by his side around the clock, for as long as it took for his life to stabilize. And that's what I had done for almost two weeks, only leaving him in the care of our roommate when I headed into work. But that night, my brother's last night, he fell asleep on the couch. He looked... peaceful. So I thought I'd head to the gym."

I swallow back the tears that well behind my eyes. "I was stressed too. I was a twenty-something with the weight of the world on my shoulders and I wanted to forget for a while. I left my cell phone in the gym locker and tuned out the world. I didn't see his texts. I took my time. Ran. Lifted. Headed to the sauna. My brother called over and over. In the end, I missed seven calls from him. Seven chances to talk him into making a better decision." I shake my head.

"What happened?" Her question comes out through clenched teeth.

"Apparently my brother woke up more depressed than ever. From what they were able to piece together, he got in his truck and headed to a liquor store." My hands tremble. "Then he went and parked in the woods. He drank everything he bought. When he tried to find his way out, he didn't make it. Wrapped his truck around a tree instead." As I relive the worst night of my life for the first time in a long time, my forehead beads with sweat.

She leans in toward me but I scoot away from her. I want to take in the look on her face before I tell her the rest of the story and everything between us changes.

The warm glow of the outdoor light illuminates the round of her cheeks. With her eyebrows arched and her mouth pursed together in a sympathetic line, Stella is the picture of compassion. This may be the last time she ever looks at me with such kindness.

"I'm sorry, that's terrible. That isn't your fault." Stella's voice is sweet.

"I should have been there. But if that part is up for debate, the next part isn't. I hadn't yet heard that something awful had happened to my brother, but I knew in my heart that something was off. I felt it in my core that the only person I'd ever loved with my whole heart was gone." A tear burns hot on the side of my face.

"You don't have to tell me anymore. It's okay," Stella reaches for my hand but I pull away.

"I was in a full panic by the time I pulled into the driveway. As I tried to piece together where my brother had gone, I interrogated our roommate. He told me that my brother *planned* to drink. He *planned* to head to the woods. He *planned* to throw away everything he had been working toward." My heartbeat ticks up just thinking about it. "Our roommate was drunk himself. He tossed my brother the keys to his truck. Gave him fifty bucks. Told him to have a round of drinks." I press my hand to my forehead.

"Roman... What'd you do?" Stella's eyes go wide and her voice is barely above a whisper.

"I lost control. I don't know exactly because I blacked out, to be honest. It's a blur. Before I could think, my fist was on his face. My body was vibrating with anger. I remember being on top of him. I was seeing red. I didn't stop until the cops were pulling me off him, locking me into the back of a police car. I didn't kill him, but I would have if they hadn't shown up. Absolutely. Without a doubt. As it was, he was hurt badly. Bad enough for me to spend a fair amount of time in prison."

Stella's jaw drops open and I nod. This is the reaction I deserve.

"It's where I deserved to be. I managed to strike a deal that allowed me to have my records sealed so that I work without having to register as a felon. But they can seal everything they want, I know what I did and now you do too. That's what your brother's report will say when they uncover it." I slide my chair away from the table.

I watch as a thousand barely detectable shades of emotion wash across Stella's face. Fine lines wrinkle at the corners of her eyes. Most of them are unreadable, but there are a few emotions that float to the surface loud and clear. Shock. Sadness. Concern.

I give it a few minutes. But when Stella stays resolute in her silence, I put us both out of our misery and get to my feet.

"I don't want you to be uncomfortable in your own house. I bet you don't want me anywhere you, or McKenna at this point. I don't blame you for that, I'm only sorry I let this get out of hand. I'm sorry." I take a cautious step toward the glass door and Stella stands in what I assume is stunned silence.

Her eyes are wide and blinking, her lips part ever so slightly. "Stop. Don't leave. I just need a minute. In the past, I've made a habit of falling for bad guys who pretend to be good. But I know your heart. I think you are a good guy pretending to be bad."

She takes a step toward me and puts her hand in mine. When I try to pull away, she squeezes even tighter.

"I'm sorry for what you've been through. I can't imagine. Shawn lost his son a few years back and he was cast into a pit of despair so dark I think he may have done the same thing if he was given the chance."

I wipe a tear from my face. How is it possible that instead of recoiling away from me, Stella is showering me with a grace I've never been able to extend to myself?

I shake my head. "No, you don't have to do this. I know who I am—"

"You are such a strong man." Stella wraps her arms around me.

It isn't often that I let myself fall apart. But I don't think about that now. Instead, I relax into the warmth of her embrace. I kiss the top of her head and inhale her sweet, floral, scent. I don't know how long I'll get to hold her like this but I'm going to take advantage of every second.

When she pulls away, I take her by the shoulders. "I already told your brother everything about my past. But I also told him that I've fallen in love with a beautiful woman who is way out of my league. I made a promise that after tonight I'd leave you alone forever. But before I go, I wanted to make sure I got McKenna's playhouse put together. That's what we were doing in your yard."

I hold out my hand to her and Stella takes it. She isn't hesitant in the way I'm half-expecting her to be. Instead, she's warm. Squeezing my hand and blinking up at me with teary eyes as I lead her out to the playhouse.

When we walk around the corner, I hold my arm to present the mostly finished project. "When I saw that piece of junk that was waiting to be assembled, I couldn't help but make a few improvements on it."

Illuminated by two rows of Christmas lights overhead, the two-story, A-frame playhouse with red shutters stands proud. The window planter boxes are full of bright flowers and the second story window has a bucket on a pulley system. Attached to the back is a covered space with a hammock, swing, slide, and tiny greenhouse.

"Wow, this is incredible. I don't believe it." Stella's eyes dart around the space taking it all in.

"The hammock is actually for adults. I thought you might want a place to read out here while she plays. Oh, and the greenhouse so you can grow food all year round for McKenna to serve up in her cafe." I rub the tight muscles on the back of my neck.

"That is so thoughtful. I can't believe this is my yard. I don't know how you transformed my little patch of icy grass into a dreamland for my daughter and me, but thank you."

I spend the next ten minutes showing her all the thoughtful details. Stella covers her mouth in surprise after each one. When I can't possibly think of any more reasons to stall, I bring the back of her hand to my mouth and plant a soft kiss on it.

"I won't stick around. I just wanted you to know that you've shown me a side of myself I didn't know existed and I will be grateful to you for the rest of my life. I want you to find someone who treats you like the queen you are, someone who will protect your heart. Can you do that for me?"

I wait, heart pounding in my chest for Stella to shrug away from me. To look at me in horror with shock and disdain. But she doesn't. Instead, Stella leans into my side.

"I've already found him." Stella puts her head on my shoulder. "I wish you would have told me sooner. I'm so sorry you went through something so gut-wrenching. When we lost my nephew, it was devastating for our entire family. Shawn leaned on us to get through it and I can't imagine having to shoulder that kind of grief all alone."

"It doesn't matter how many people you do or don't have. It's all hard." I put an arm over her shoulder.

"Roman, you have a past, but together we can make a future that looks like anything we want it to. You aren't your choices. You're a good man who deserves a second chance. You can't live your life trying to bring your brother back but you can honor his memory by making a new future. Can you do that for me?"

"I can." I choke my words out in an almost whisper and pull Stella into my arms. "I can do it *with* you."

When she looks up at me, I catch her chin in my hand and plant my mouth on hers. The kiss bubbles through me and I feel the rush of a promise of forever.

After my brother passed, I lost my vision for my future. But with Stella in my arms, I'm filled with the hope that I might somehow carve out a new one.

I know deep within me that this kiss could be the start of a new chapter, one I undoubtedly don't deserve. But if she's willing to take a chance on me, I'll earn her love one day at a time.

As I hold her, the sound of footsteps on the back porch catches my attention, but Stella doesn't move. She stays still, face buried into my chest. When Shawn pops his head around the corner, I look at him over the top of her head.

He freezes and takes in the sight. Then, Shawn gives me a head nod and walks back out without saying a single word. I hear the rumble of his truck pulling out of her driveway.

He trusts me. *She* trusts me.

Tears rush out of my eyes as I realize that when it comes to Stella, I can trust myself. There isn't anything I won't do for this precious woman.

Chapter Twelve: Stella

Six Months Later

That Christmas, Carole Cat did get a home for Christmas, ours. Between the addition of our white kitty to our world, and the fact that Roman hardly ever goes home, life sure looks different these days. Our little house that used to feel empty with only McKenna and me in it, is now brimming with love, warmth, and things that work properly.

Sometimes I have to pinch myself. It's like I'm walking around waiting for the other shoe to drop with Roman. He seems too good to be true. Yet, he's real and flawed in the most beautiful ways.

Roman has shown up for McKenna and me day after day. Making us smile. Cooking our, meals. Coming with me to McKenna's school activities. It's nothing extravagant, but it's invaluable.

When it's just the two of us, Roman ravages my body. He worships my curves and loves every part of me. The way he makes me feel is simply beyond anything I ever dreamed of for myself.

A summer breeze hits my face as I look out of my kitchen window and into my backyard. The warm sun casts a golden glow over everything. I can't help but smile because the playhouse Roman constructed gets plenty of use and today is no exception.

"Can I take your order? You know we do have blueberry muffins." McKenna puts her hand to her mouth and drops her voice to a whisper. "For real, they're in the kitchen. I can bring one out."

Roman looks like a giant with his knees crammed into his chest as he sits in the chair across from McKenna. My cheeks flush with warmth as I take in their adorable relationship. It seems like a dream. In Roman, McKenna has the father she deserves. She may not have his eyes, but without a doubt, she has his heart.

"In that case, I'll take two." Roman bites back a smile. "Oh, and miss, while you're in the kitchen, maybe a little something for my friend here please?" Roman gestures to Carole Cat, and McKenna breaks into a full grin.

"No problem sir, coming right up." McKenna skips inside, Carole Cat hot on her heels. "Mom, I have a customer at my cafe. I need two blueberry muffins and I need something for Carole Cat. Probably just a cat treat now that I think about it..." McKenna rambles as she loads up a tray. "Oh, and can I have this picture?"

McKenna reaches up and plucks the picture of me sitting on Santa's lap from the office Christmas party.

"Hey, careful, that is special." I love to relive that night in my mind. It was the night I knew without a doubt that I loved Roman.

"I know, I want to put them on the wall in my cafe. That way I can look at it while I'm cooking. I like Roman's silly Santa outfit." McKenna runs her finger down the photo strip.

"And my ugly sweater?" I laugh.

"No, I like your smile. You look so happy."

A lump swells in my throat looking back on the night that started it all. "That picture is special, you should put it up in the playhouse for sure."

"Thanks, Mom!"

Epilogue: Stella

Ten Months Later

Roman proposed to me just a few weeks after our office Christmas party at Brew by Brewer. But I wasn't ready to say yes. It's strange to look back on that time in my life. I knew deep down he was my person from the very start but I still fought it a bit.

I was gun-shy given what I had been through only a few months prior to our meeting. But somehow, Roman was okay with all that came with being in my life.

Instead of pushing me into a commitment with him, Roman played the long game. He stood back and gave me space even when it was painful for him. He showed me what it means to love selflessly, staying steady in his resolve to be a rock in my life. It's just one of the many things that made me fall for him.

Roman brought me breakfast in bed. He fixed the things in my house that I didn't even know were broken. He won over my parents. He worked to develop a friendship with my brother Shawn even though Shawn didn't make it easy in the beginning.

Best of all, Roman put in the time to get to know McKenna. I don't always understand where her dad's head is at. But I feel sorry for Spencer. He's missing out on the most amazing little girl. I wish their relationship was different. But watching Roman come into her life and fill that gap in my daughter's life warms my heart in a way I'll never have enough words to explain.

Without a doubt, Roman has proved one million times in one million little ways that he is exactly who I hoped he'd be. Simply put, he's the man of my dreams. Every single sacrifice and bump in the road along the way was worth it to arrive at my place by his side.

Roman stayed steady in his resolve not to pressure me. But as the weeks passed, I ran out of reasons not to say yes. And in the end, McKenna and I invited Roman over for dinner where we proposed to him.

Roman couldn't hold back the tears that streamed down his cheeks. But through them, he managed to choke out a resounding *yes*. The rest is history.

Today I'm standing in the back of the chapel at the Brew by Brewer Resort. This time, there aren't any Halloween costumes. Now that the man is right, everything else seems unnecessary.

My mother thought getting married in the same place my last wedding imploded was bad luck, but I disagree. For all the hurt Spencer caused me, my connection to the Brewer family has given me some of the things I love most in this world. My job. My daughter, and now, my husband.

The last time I was in this position, I was wracked with nerves. Stomach clenching and my heart pounding in my chest. Today, those feelings are gone.

Starting my new life in the same place my old one ended feels like poetic justice. We built our foundation on the ashes of the broken promises of my last relationship, so this seems right.

Now it's just me in a white dress ready to walk down the aisle toward the man who has changed my life in every way. Standing at the back of this chapel, ready to walk toward my forever, all I feel is happy.

I draw in a slow and steady breath. It seems I'm not the only one feeling decidedly more confident. The music starts and I begin my walk, a bouquet of white calla lilies clutched in my hands.

As I look out at the small gathering of family and friends, my brother Shawn beams at me. Knowing Roman and I have his blessing warms me from the inside out.

When I get to the front of the chapel, Roman takes his hands in mine. His eyes go glassy. When he runs his thumbs across the back of my hands, it makes my heart skip a beat.

As our ceremony moves forward, the officiant asks for my vows. When I turn to Roman, I can hardly speak through my tears. "I trust you with my whole heart. Thank you for being an incredible man and thank you for loving me. I promise to show you every day that you are my favorite person."

When it's Roman's turn to say his vows, he swallows hard. "Stella, I don't deserve you. But for some reason I can't understand, you're here. I promise to love you, protect you, and cherish you for all my life. Loving you is my biggest accomplishment and I'll spend my life making sure you know that."

Roman's words dance in my heart and fill me with joy. They are the sweetest I've ever heard. Before the ceremony continues, Roman holds up his hand. "There's one more thing I need to say."

"What are you doing?" I whisper.

"McKenna honey, come over here." Roman drops to his knees and takes her seven-year-old hand in his, I swallow the lump in my throat. "I didn't get to see your first steps or rock you to sleep at night. But you have my heart. You're my girl and I love you. I promise you that I will take care of you, I'll be on your side, and I'll help you get anything you want in this world. I never knew what it would be like to be a parent, but my heart grew when I met you and I'm so lucky."

Roman pulls McKenna into a tight hug and the tears that have been welling up behind my eyes spill over at the sight. I can't help but feel overwhelmed with gratitude for the example Roman will set in McKenna's life. She will never have to wonder about her worth.

As the officiant pronounces us husband and wife, Roman interlaces his fingers with mine. Roman isn't the man I thought I'd end up with. He's messy and complicated. But somehow he's a perfect fit for me, rough in all the right places.

We share our first kiss as husband and wife to an eruption of applause inconsistent with the small number of friends and family gathered in front of us. Roman holds up our hands to the crowd and McKenna lets out a cheer of excitement.

Roman reaches down and scoops her up. The three of us walk out of the chapel together, a family heading into our happily ever after.

Love Struck, Chapter One: Hannah

I swallow the last drink of my third pink, sugar-rimmed cocktail and eat the red candy heart garnish that came on top. Then I grab another as I make my way around the room. It's the night of the aptly named Brew by Brewer Worst Day of the Year Valentine's party.

I've never been lucky in love and I don't even work at Brew by Brewer. Yet somehow I've found myself here wearing my sister Kaylee's name tag. As it turns out this party is doing its best to live up to its title.

The clubhouse attached to the golf course at Brew by Brewer is nice inside and certainly large enough to hold the two hundred employees who are here tonight. But the decor isn't doing anything to help the cheese factor. The walls are adorned with enormous naked babies holding bows and arrows.

Apparently, the entire event planning team is out on maternity leave at Brew by Brewer. So planning this Valentine's party for singles was left entirely up to the happily married men of the Brewer family. Alas, tons of naked cupids.

If I had to guess, I'd say someone did an internet search for Valentine's party ideas and just did all of them. There's wine, chocolate-covered strawberries, an incredible number of stuffed teddy bears, and games fit for a middle school dance. I laugh to myself. This party is just one more thing that is not quite right for me about Misty Mountain.

When my sister Kaylee moved here to be with her fiancé, Shawn, I felt that I didn't have any choice other than to come with her. She and I have been a package deal all our lives. I've helped her raise my niece, Rosie since she was a baby.

My sister is my whole world and I can't imagine my life without her. When we lost my parents, Kaylee was barely an adult herself. I was still a child without any options. My sister chose to sacrifice her twenties to raise me and she did a good job of it too.

I didn't make it easy either. My sister has had to endure meeting one train wreck of a boyfriend after the next. I always go for the guys who want to change me. But through it all, Kaylee's been there steadfast and solid.

"Hey, aren't you a tall drink of water?" A drunk mountain man slurs his words in my direction and I shake my head.

"Nope. No thanks." I slip past him and he latches onto my arm.

"Come on sweetheart, I'm single and ready to mingle."

"Have a good night." I rip my arm away from him and head to the bar for another cocktail.

That's Misty Mountain's finest for you.

Cheesy eighties music plays as I search for somewhere else to be. Anywhere else. I take my drink and step out of the backdoor, wandering into a massive covered garage lined with golf carts. I check the ignitions, no keys. Too bad, that could have really turned my night around.

I can't leave yet. Kaylee is really hoping I'll fall in love with this place. Truthfully, I hope so too. It'd be so much easier. I don't hate this small town. But with Kaylee and Shawn settled and expecting their first child, they spend their time with Shawn's sister Stella and her new fiancé Roman who also have a child, McKenna.

I'm thrilled to see my sister happy and living the life she deserves. But the foursome has left me feeling like a shadow in someone else's life. I mean, they're all together right now, having a game night. Meanwhile,

I'm here at a single's party for employees of a company where I don't even work.

I wander through the garage. Its dull, massive gray walls depict exactly how I feel. I stumble across a maintenance cart, inside are four cans of paint. I think of the letter I received earlier tucked into the top drawer of my dresser and shake the thought away.

Attending art school would definitely be a change of pace, but is it the right change of pace? My sister would be devastated if I left this town.

I stare at the paint cans, my stomach in knots. Then I make a snap decision. Art school may not be in my future, but I think I'm just the right amount of drunk to paint some life onto these walls. I throw back my red martini with the pink sugar rim and pick up a paintbrush to get to work.

This may be the drinks talking, but I think that whoever has to *see* these walls will really appreciate my talent. Besides, there's nothing else for me to do at this party. It's my contribution to Brew by Brewer.

"You. Are. Welcome," I say aloud to myself. I dip my paintbrush in a thick, bright red can of paint then splatter it onto the wall. "Lovely. Better already."

A half-hour later, the wall is unrecognizable. Of course, there isn't a ton I can do with only a few colors, but keeping with the theme of the evening an enormous red heart seems appropriate. I'm flinging paint all over the wall and all over myself too.

"This party is amazing!" I find I quite like the sound of my echo off the tall ceilings. "Happy Worst Day of the Year Party to me." I'm lost in a moment of creative bliss, giggling and laughing to myself in an alcohol-fueled stupor. "Be my Valentine."

"Okay, if you're asking." The deep growl of a man's voice behind me makes me sober up immediately.

My blood runs cold. When I turn to face him, my knees go weak. He's tall with broad shoulders, a chiseled jawline, and the most smoldering brown eyes I've ever seen. All I can do is stand here like an idiot, mouth hanging open and mind racing.

Shit.

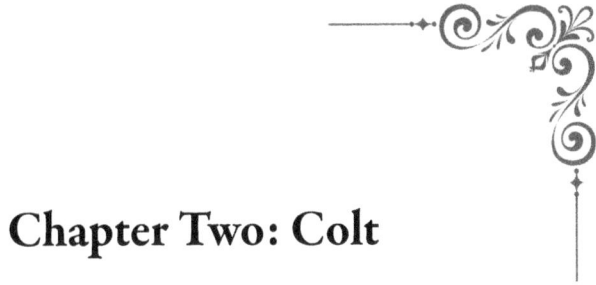

Chapter Two: Colt

"Shit. Shit." She repeats herself. "You scared me. I didn't see you there." The woman looks down and a beautiful flush of red crawls across her cheeks then down her neck. My eyes trail down the top of her dress and I can't help but wonder where it stops.

"No, you don't have to stop. I like it... it's interesting. You've got a little paint on your dress. But this place needed some sparkle if you ask me." My eyes drift to her nametag. "Kaylee... Allen of the cat cafe, hmm." I bite back a smile. She doesn't look anything like the Kaylee Allen I know and I wonder where she got the nametag. "Do you work here then?"

"I umm. Yes, I work here... of course. Why else would I be here? I work right over there." She points in one direction and then the other. "There, you know, over at the cat cafe. I make cakes and stuff with cats. I mean, not with cats, that sounded weird. Like, they don't cook in there or have tiny aprons or anything." She smoothes the long pink skirt of her dress. "But they thought they needed a little color so they sent me here to uh, paint tonight."

She is a terrible liar, adorable, but terrible.

"Is that so?" My mouth pulls into a sideways smirk. "And who are *they* if you don't mind me asking?"

Fake-Kaylee crosses her arms over her chest and turns her nose up at me. "I do mind. But if you have to know, the Brewer brothers. They've hired me."

"Ah, yes... to paint the golf course and cook with cats," I repeat, wondering how long it will take her to come clean.

"Correct."

"Then, by all means, let me help you." I take a step closer to her, pick up a paintbrush, and hurl a dollop of pink paint onto the concrete wall.

Fake-Kaylee's eyes widen. "Um, the manager of the golf course is pretty intense from what I hear. You might not want to do that. I'm working from a template here."

"He probably won't mind." I splatter more paint. "By the way Kaylee, how's your daughter Rosie? Just wanted to check in about her. You see, you look a lot different than the last time I saw you. So I just wanted to make sure that everything is okay at home."

The woman stands up straight and she lets out a long exhale. "Okay, you got me. I may have had one too many of these drinks with the sugar rims and the candy hearts. I'm Hannah Allen. I just moved here with my sister, Kaylee. She works at the cat cafe. She wasn't using her ticket to the party tonight so she thought maybe I should come in her place. You know, meet some decent people. Get to know the area." She picks up a paintbrush and rounds out the edges and lines of the massive heart in her mural.

"Ah, I know the cat cafe well, my buddy Roman kind of has a thing for one of the ladies who works up there. They are actually engaged now," I say.

"Let me guess, her name is Stella?" Hannah stays focused on her painting and I wonder if she's really that enthralled with her work or if she's just trying to sober up.

"It is, she's got a daughter—" I start.

"McKenna. Yes, I know. I'm her nanny. I watch my niece Rosie too. They're the same age."

"Is that right?" I make a mental note to ask Roman why he's been holding out information about the sexy as hell nanny they're employing.

"Yeah, but I really am an artist too. I mean, I probably shouldn't be doing this, no one told me I could. But it will look good when I'm done better than the gray and I can't exactly go back now." She bites her lip when she pauses and I'm mesmerized.

Hannah rambles as her beautiful sequin gown with the flowing skirt is splattered with paint. I learn that she's single with a history of picking the wrong guys. I learn that she hopes to take adventures but for some reason feels guilty about it.

She doesn't seem drunk anymore, just honest. More than that, I can tell Hannah doesn't care at all about appearances. Maybe that's why I can't stop watching her. She's stunning with delicate features, long hair, and curves in all the right places. But it's more than that.

There's something so free about the way she moves. My eyes trace the outline of her curves in her sparkling gown. She's intoxicating and unlike anyone I've ever met. Without another thought, I pick up a paintbrush and paint a massive stroke of color across the wall. It's awful and out of place. But it gets her attention, and that was the goal.

Hannah's head whips toward me. "What are you doing?" Her words don't have any bite to them.

"Helping you." I paint another massive line.

"That looks terrible." She smiles at me, eyebrows raised. "You're getting it everywhere."

"No, *now* I'm getting it everywhere." I take my paintbrush and tap it on her arm.

Hannah's mouth drops open in surprise and her eyes go wide. It only takes a second for her to respond by hitting me with her own blob of paint. From there, we erupt into a frenzy of paint and laughter.

Within minutes we are entangled with each other, wrestling, tugging, and flirting. Sparks fly back and forth between us. The wall is a wreck and so are we. When Hannah stumbles on her gown, I catch her in my arms, but she takes me to the ground with her.

She lets out a yelp, but I've got her, safe in my arms. I hold her there, breathless with laughter. Hannah looks up at me, the golden flecks in her eyes reflecting the light. I swear she's the most gorgeous woman I've ever seen.

Her lips purse into a straight line. "So what do you do besides corner women in vacant rooms and cover them in paint?"

I can't take my eyes off her pouty pink lips and I inch ever closer to her face.

"I was a professional golfer. Spent a few years on the tour, but I'm past that point in my life. So now I'm back here where I grew up. Holding the most beautiful woman I've ever seen in my arms while she's covered in paint." I watch the swell of her chest heave up and down. "I'm going to have to thank your sister for giving you her ticket."

"She's trying to give me a reason to love Misty Mountain and want to stay here forever." Hannah looks into my eyes, reaches up, and puts a hand on my cheek.

"I'm Colt Calloway. I run the golf course here at Brew by Brewer. I didn't hire anyone to paint a mural, but I might be able to give you a reason to like Misty Mountain."

With that, I can't take it anymore. Instinct takes over. I close my eyes and plant my mouth on hers. It sends heat coursing through every inch of my body. When I part her lips with my tongue I swear fireworks erupt between us.

There's electricity in her touch and I don't mind the shock. Holding her, kissing her, it makes my heart pound in my chest. Our tongues dance. Our hands roam. I'm taken with her, overwhelmed with the need to claim Hannah as my own. I never want this moment to end. But when I put a hand on the curve of her hip, she opens her eyes to look up at me.

Her voice is a soft whisper. "Before we go any further, you need to know that I'm leaving. I won't be in Misty Mountain for long, I don't think. I'm going to disappoint a lot of people and I don't want to add you to the list."

I shake my head. "You're not leaving tonight are you?"

"No," she says.

"That's enough for me." Thankfully I'm a better liar than she is.

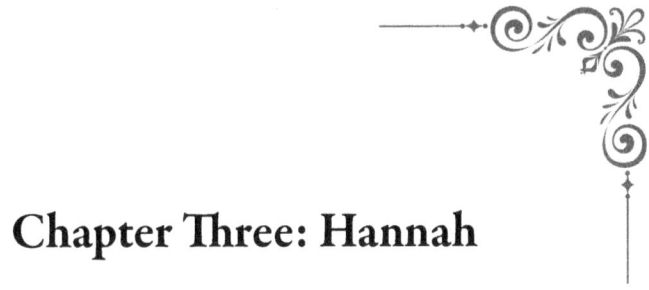

Chapter Three: Hannah

Without another thought, I plant my lips back on his. He uses his tongue to part my mouth and it draws a sharp breath from me. I've sobered up, but I get drunk on the electricity zapping between us. In an instant, his mouth is on my neck. Colt's kisses come hard and fast.

Things move in a frenzy of wild heat from there. One minute, I'm straddling Colt in a golf cart. The next he's pulling me down some back hallway attached to the clubhouse. Everywhere I look are dark oak floors and black leather furniture.

When we fall through the door of an abandoned office, he closes it behind us. Colt wraps his hand around my throat, shoving me backward and pinning me to the wall. He's in charge and I fucking love it. His hands roam my curves leaving a trail of heat in their wake and I want more.

He wraps one hand around my wrists, immobilizing me while the other grasps at my ass, palming my cheek and smacking it until it stings. I feel the bulge in his pants twitch hard against me. The weight of his body pressed against mine makes me ache with desire.

I rock my hips into him and the sensation sends fiery tingles coursing through my body. When he lifts me off the ground, I wrap my thighs tightly around my waist, desperate for more friction. I put my arms around his neck and tug at the hair on the base of his neck. When I do, Colt buries his face in my cleavage.

He pulls down the sequin corset top of my dress and peppers my breasts with kisses. I take in the tantalizing scent of leather as he nuzzles into me, I can't tell if it's him or the furniture. But it's hard to care when his tongue is circling my nipple until it constricts into a tight eraser tip.

Warmth blooms low in me, flooding my body and making my panties drenched. Colt's kisses are desperate. A visceral longing for him curls in my stomach. I can tell he's hungry for me and I can't wait to give myself to him.

When Colt steps away, tugging me toward the overstuffed black sofa, I follow without complaint. Before I can sit, he slides up behind me, pushing me forward at the waist. I pillow my head with my arms. Colt's hand hooks around me. He hitches the long skirt of my dress up around my waist, reaching for my panties. When he finds them, he tugs them down in a swift movement.

His fingers run along the slit of my already slick opening. He moves across my folds with expert precision. My clit is already swollen and engorged. When he plunges inside, I'm all but begging for more. Every movement pulls another faint plea from my lips. He's stretched me open and now I'm desperate to be filled.

Colt spreads my thighs with his knee and I'm all too happy to let my legs fall open for him. My face is buried in the couch and my ass is turned up toward him. I feel the tip of his length knock at my opening. Tiny tremors run up and down my body, I'm desperate to let him in, slippery with excitement.

He pauses for a moment, pulsating against me. Throbbing. Making me ache for him. When he enters me, Colt does so with a single heavy thrust of his hips and I take all of him. My walls stretch around him and he pulsates inside of me.

His hands land firmly on the swell of my ass. He squeezes so hard I wonder if he'll leave handprints. A part of me hopes he does. I'm his now, at least for the night. As Colt pumps into me, my breasts bob and bounce in time with his every movement.

He reaches forward, moving a hand over my breasts and rolling my nipples between his fingers. As he pushes even deeper inside of me. I lean back into his thrusts, meeting him with all my momentum. The smolder between us ignites into a full flame.

We pick up the pace, making a sound echo in time with each plunge. He wraps his hand in a fistful of my hair and jerks my head back. His mouth lands on the sensitive skin on the side of my neck. A low guttural groan leaves his lips.

My breathy moans of pleasure build with each thrust. I can't help it, I push back into him, rocking my hips to meet him, hungry for more of the beautiful friction. I arch my back, clenching along his length. My movements send him deeper into my abyss.

Hot tidal waves of pleasure course through me and it takes my breath away. He puts his hands on my waist and slams into me. Mountainous tremors build in sync with his movements and my breath goes erratic. My body quivers as my walls threaten to collapse along his length. I bear down on him, moaning his name.

"Hannah, you're gonna make me lose it. Fuck. Oh, fuck." He grunts strangled words and he flexes his muscles.

The sensation pushes me over the edge. When I let go, I cover my mouth. But it does nothing to stifle the loud scream of release that pierces the night air as it forces its way through my lips. I spasm. My walls collapse along his still hard length. My chest heaves and my lips pant his name. It's only one more mighty thrust before Colt is shooting into me and I'm milking him to the last drop.

We lay there, lost in each other, basking in the afterglow of the best sex on the worst day of the year.

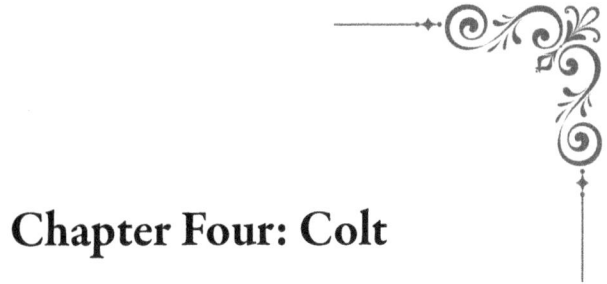

Chapter Four: Colt

Hannah and I step back into the party hand in hand. My buzz is gone, but I'm drunk on Hannah. I've never met anyone like her. She's beautiful, uninhibited, and free. She isn't tied to an idea of what people think she should be and it's so refreshing. Not to mention I just had the most mind-blowing sex of my life. With her by my side, I feel somehow closer to the man I want to be and I can't get enough.

"Come on, we're pinning the arrow on cupid." I take her hand in mine and pull Hannah toward the crowd. "But I'm getting you a drink first."

"Only if it's topped with a sugary heart." She follows, her body draped over mine like the missing piece of a puzzle.

It's incredible how different this party feels with Hannah by my side. The room which looked cheesy and drab comes to life in vibrant colors. Covered in paint and wrapped in the blissful afterglow of amazing sex, I'm sure we stand out in the crowd. When we get to the bar, I bypass the line and walk behind it.

"Perks of running the clubhouse." I wink at her.

"Okay, I'm into that," Hannah laughs.

"What do we have here? I'm surprised to see you looking so cozy with... Kaylee, is it?" My father's voice punctures my blissful bubble and I straighten. "This can't be the young lady who will pass along the family name. Can it?"

I roll my eyes. "Dad, this is Hannah Allen. She's got on her sister's name tag. There won't ever be anyone passing along the family name as long as you put so much pressure on everyone who comes into contact with me." I shake my head.

"Nice to meet you, Hannah." My father's eyes run up and down Hannah's paint-stricken dress. His jaw clenches in a telltale sign of his disapproval, though I'm sure she didn't notice. My eyes have been trained to look for the subtle signs in him over the years. "Very creative outfit."

I know he's trying to make her uncomfortable, it's his way and it makes me cringe. But Hannah looks up at him and she doesn't look embarrassed. Her shoulders are back and her head is held high.

Her mouth pulls into a dazzling smile. "Thank you so much. I was going to suggest a little pink paint to spice up your jacket. I think I could find some. Get you looking festive."

My eyes widen at Hannah's response. *Is she going toe to toe with him? This isn't going to end well.*

But when I look at Dad, his mouth pulls into a smile. "Is that so?" He doesn't seem angry at all. If anything, he looks amused, charmed even.

"I can tell you're the kind of man who wants to keep with the times. Paint dresses are all the rage." She winks. "Your son gets it and I tell you two have a lot in common. You must be where Colt gets his good looks."

Winks... At my father... While she's covered in paint.

"She's kidding Dad, she—" I stop.

My mouth falls open in shock as Dad lets out a deep, throaty chuckle. "You think so? Oh man, I tell you what, watch out for this one, son. She's a firecracker." Dad claps me on the back with a nod of approval. "Now that Colt here isn't a pro-golfer anymore, it's high time he moves on with his life. We've been waiting on him to join the firm. Either that or pick up a club again."

"I don't know that I like golf anymore. You'll have to dig deep and find something else you like to brag about." I let out a humorless chuckle. My parents have strong ideas about what my life should look like, a marriage, a house, a baby, and a career with the family investment firm. But I'm not sure I want any of it, at least not right now.

"Better pick up a club again then. Hannah, it was a pleasure," Dad says. He makes his way back into the crowd, whiskey in hand.

That could have gone so much worse. I look at Hannah, she seems unphased by the interaction. Which is impressive seeing as my Dad has a habit of reducing people to tears regularly.

"So... that's your dad. Seems like a sweetheart." She raises an eyebrow at me and there's a hint of sarcasm in her voice which makes me like her that much more.

"Ah, my parents. They're good old Misty Mountain royalty. Been together since they were kids and have never looked back. Now they're retired and waiting on me to make them grandparents. No pressure, right?" I let out a rough chuckle. "You handled him like a champ."

"Does he always put that much pressure on you? And what the hell is the firm? It sounds so ominous."

"Yes, since before I can remember. And the firm is my father's investment firm. It operates on the good old boy's network and I don't want any part of it," I say.

"I can see that." Hannah gives me a shrug and a smile. "Maybe we should get back to this worst night of the year affair. Is that my drink?" She gestures to the pink, sugar-rimmed glass in my hand.

"You know it." I hand it over and Hannah takes a long sip off the top.

"Let's go, that game is calling our names. Besides, I can hardly wait to blindfold you." I growl my words into her ear then steer Hannah toward the pin-the-heart-on-cupid game.

Hannah throws back the rest of her drink and rocks up onto her tiptoes. "Tonight I'm all yours but there's one rule I won't break. At the end of this, we're not exchanging numbers. I'm not going to be here for much longer and falling for you will only complicate things."

"So you're falling for me." I wrap my arms around her. "That's what I like to hear."

A red blush crawls across her cheeks. "I mean it. Tonight is the end of this. I got accepted to an art school on the coast and I'm probably going to go. If not, then I'm at least getting out of here and finding an adventure or two. But I don't know when I'll be back, if ever. So I can't start anything serious with you. It's going to be hard enough to leave. It's tonight only, do we have a deal?" She looks into my eyes.

"Hell no. I hate that plan." I cup the curve of her ass with my palms.

"Colt, I'm not giving you my number. Maybe if it's meant to be, we'll just find our way back to each other." She chews on her bottom lip and it drives me wild.

"That's fine, keep your number to yourself. It's a small town and I like a challenge. I'll hunt you down Joe Goldberg style if that's what you're into."

She shakes her head at me with a laugh. "That's definitely not what I'm into."

"Tell me what you're into then, because I'm into curvy women in sequin dresses, covered in paint."

Hannah and I spend the rest of the night lost in each other. We drink, dance, and play every single cheesy game available. I kiss her every chance I get. I study the outline of her curves in her dress and commit every single one of them to memory. There's something about this girl that tells me my life won't ever be the same.

But when the night ends and I walk her to her car, Hannah keeps her word. She leaves me with only the memory of what I already know is the best night of my life. But it isn't enough for me, I want more of her. In fact, I want all of her.

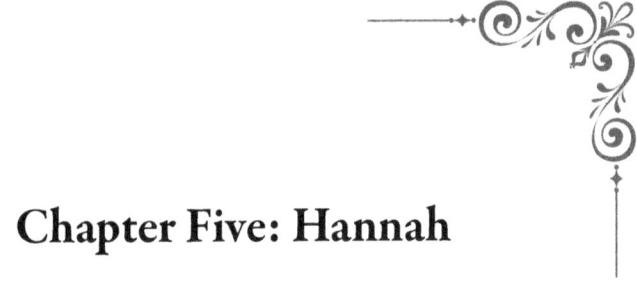

Chapter Five: Hannah

Not exchanging contact information with Colt was maybe the most responsible decision I've made in a very long time. But not having a way to contact him hasn't done anything for keeping my mind from wandering back through the memory of our night together. He's all I've been able to think about and it's left me feeling lower than ever.

"Can we talk?" Kaylee leans against my kitchen counter, keys still in hand.

I've been avoiding my sister since I went to the Valentine's party as her, got drunk, painted an unwarranted mural, and had sex in a clubhouse a few days ago. "Sure?" My stomach clenches under her stare and I try to keep my voice casual.

"Well, funny thing. I was at work and I heard that someone painted a drunken mural at Brew by Brewer wearing a nametag with my name on it."

Shit.

My sister has just settled into her job at the Brew by Brewer Cat Cafe and the last thing I want is to mess that up for her. "Yeah, about that, the party was pretty terrible and I got a little restless. I... I don't have any excuse actually and I'm sorry. I hope I didn't cause too many issues for you."

Kaylee holds up her hand. "No, you don't have to apologize. Lucy Brewer, one of the owners saw it and she loved it. Word got around that I did it and she came into the cafe looking to chat with me about the possibility of painting more. It was a little awkward when I had to explain that it wasn't exactly me. But she was a great sport about it."

I blow out a sigh of relief. "Thank goodness. I was worried that was going to be the end of you working at the cat cafe."

"No, in fact, it's such good news. The Brewer family wants to hire you to paint more murals." Kaylee claps her hands and shifts her weight back and forth between her feet the way she does when she's excited. "Isn't that incredible? A job, doing art, right here in Misty Mountain. It's kind of the best of all worlds. What do you think?"

"Yeah, wow. That's awesome."

And it is awesome, I think. But for some reason, the heaviness returns to my chest anyway. I don't know why exactly. It could be a really good setup, I suppose. Being paid for my art has always been a dream of mine. But there's something about this that doesn't sit well with me. It's one more tether holding me to a life in Misty Mountain that I'm not sure I want. It's silly really, I should be excited.

"Okay, good. I thought you'd be happy about it. Since Roman oversees the grounds, he thought maybe he could take you with him to work on Monday. He'd show you the ropes and get you set up with your first project."

"Monday? That's so soon." My throat runs dry thinking about the commitment.

"I know, right? And the best part is they're letting you choose your schedule so we can do this around McKenna and Rosie's school schedules if that works, which I totally think it will! I'm so excited for you." Kaylee's eyes run across my face. "What's the matter? It's exciting isn't it?" She tilts her head, eyeing me with suspicion.

"Yeah, it's great. I'm happy about that. Just didn't expect that is all. A job right here in Misty Mountain, wow." I consider what it could look like.

Could I be happy? Will that be enough for me? Why can't I just be content here? It isn't a bad life, especially compared to how hard my sisters had to work in the past just to keep us afloat.

My head is a mess for the rest of Kaylee's visit. By the time she's packing up Rosie and getting her into the car, another thought surfaces. This one makes a stupid, indulgent smile stretch across my face.

If I'm working at Brew by Brewer, will I see Colt?

BY THE TIME MONDAY rolls around, I'm a ball of nerves. I still don't know what I want to do about my acceptance into art school and I can't shake the feeling that I need an adventure outside of life on this mountain. But right now, I don't care. There's only one thing on my mind and that's the possibility of seeing Colt today.

. The memory of his kiss on my skin and his hands on my body has run through my mind every day. Now, walking across the property and knowing he's here, the air feels electrified.

I'm supposed to meet Roman at the pub on the property but I'm not even out of the parking lot before he's making his way toward me in a golf cart. There's a pang of disappointment that whips through my stomach. A part of me was hoping I could... wander around a bit before we got started. Maybe by the golf course.

"Door-to-door service, isn't this nice?" I give him a wave.

"First day on the big job, are you ready?" Roman asks as he pulls up next to me and I slide into his golf cart beside him.

"Yeah. This is a nice place in the daylight. I couldn't see much of it at the party. What do you do here, exactly? I know Stella said you manage the facility, but what does that mean?" My eyes roam over acres of forest with old buildings scattered throughout. I can see how this would be a good place to end up. I just don't know if I'm ready to end up anywhere.

"It means I do a little of everything, fix things, clean things, build things. Whatever needs to get done. The Brewers are a good family to work for. They're fair and understanding. I think you'll like it here. Nervous?" Roman asks as we bump across the gravel road toward the main building.

"No, I'm just happy my antics at the Valentine's party ended like this and not with my sister getting in trouble." I shake my head and let out a laugh. "Do you know where I'll be painting today?" I can't help but ask the question, but I don't admit aloud that I hope he says golf course.

I've done a good job of keeping things casual with Colt up until now, mostly because I have no way of getting in touch with him. But still, for me, it's quite an accomplishment. I can admit that historically, taking things slow isn't something I'm good at.

Even though I slept with him, I silently applaud myself for my good faith effort in steering clear of him since then. I like Colt more than I'm ready to admit. But being around him can only complicate things.

I inhale and have a good chat with myself on the off chance I run into him today. *Hannah, there's a good chance you won't be here in a few weeks and you don't need another person to disappoint. I'm serious.*

Roman clears his throat and he puts a hand to the back of his neck, rolling his head from side to side. "Hey, I know I said I would show you around but I'm passing you along to my friend Colt. I uh, I think you might know him. He runs the..." Roman stops and bites back a laugh. "Yeah, I can't do this. I said I would tell you that I was sick, or make up some kind of excuse as to why I'm having him work with you today, but I can't. The truth is, the dude is dying to see you. I don't know what happened at that Valentine's party between you two and believe me, I'm not asking for details, but he's obsessed."

My cheeks flush hot and I turn my head away. But I'd be lying if I didn't say that his words thrill me. My heart rate ticks up and I suddenly wish I had spent more time getting ready. Roman pays me the kindness of not making me speak for the remainder of our drive across the property.

When we pull up at the entrance to the golf course, Roman lets me out with nothing more than a smirk. "Have a good first day."

"Thanks." I try for casual, but I'm not sure it comes across, and truthfully, why should it? I'm going to kiss Colt today.

Chapter Six: Hannah

The moment I saw him, Colt and I picked up right where we left off. He greeted me with a kiss. Not a hug. Not a handshake... a freaking kiss on the mouth. The kind where he parts my lips with his tongue and sends heat whipping through my body. I didn't stand a chance.

Two minutes in, he called me babe. Seven minutes in, he interlaced my fingers with his. If this is Colt's idea of new employee orientation, then I can't wait to see what we do once I'm actually on the clock. We're like two magnets pulled together by an invisible force. I've been with him for three hours, wandering the property and making out in corners. I haven't seen a paintbrush yet.

I start to wonder whether I actually have a job or if Colt and Roman just came up with some scheme to get me here. I tried to get started by suggesting I fix up the almost finished Valentine's mural. But when we came across the golf carts, Colt said he wanted to show me the rest of the property first. Who am I to refuse a tour? So I said I'd only go if I could drive. In retrospect, that may have been a mistake.

"Oh damn! Hannah, what the hell? Turn the wheel babe, turn!" Colt's high-pitched, exaggerated scream makes me laugh as I steer our golf cart through the woods, pedal to the floorboard. "I said left babe, left!"

"I can't stop, we'll sink into the mud!" I shout my reply through a fit of giggles.

The backwoods trail I've somehow gotten us on isn't fit for a golf cart. In fact, it isn't fit for people at all. I haven't seen a hiker for miles and I wonder if we're even still on Brewer property or just lost somewhere in the trees.

I let out an involuntary yelp as the golf cart lurches. It's barely holding up under the stress I'm applying to the tires when we come to a jerky, sliding stop only inches away from the trunk massive tree. "Ha, oh my god, I can't believe it. I didn't mean..." My chest heaves up and down as I try to recover from the shock of adrenaline.

When I turn to look at Colt, his mouth hangs open. His forehead is pinched into lines and wrinkles, and his eyes are wide. "You are the worst driver I've ever met in my life. Babe, I was a professional golfer. I've had hundreds, maybe thousands of rides in golf carts... what the hell was that?" His look of shock gives way to laughter as he teases me.

"I thought you said right, then I was committed, there wasn't any going back." I cover my mouth with my hand and I can't stop the laughter that seeps through.

"When I said let's take a tour, did you think I meant of the woods?" Colt has tears of laughter in the corners of his eyes as he throws his head back. "Ha, we're going to have to live out here now. Look at them tires, girl, those ain't going anywhere!"

I lean my head out of the driver's side and see only the tops of tires sunk deep into the sticky mud. Then I bite back a laugh, tilt my head back and yell, "help!"

"That's your plan," Colt barks his words out through his laughter. Then he cups his hands around his mouth and joins in. "Heeeelllpppp."

We take turns shouting to no one in particular in between our fits of laughter. I can't remember a time when I laughed this hard. I knew today would be an adventure, but I had no idea it'd be this much fun.

Then Colt puts a hand on my thigh and slides me toward him. "Do you do anything the normal way or is this what I should expect from now on?" His voice is low and the heat of his breath on my neck sends tingles across my body. "Hmm, what to do all alone with you, way out here where no one can see us." He runs his hand over every one of my curves, across the swell of my breasts and then between my legs.

"I can think of something," I whisper.

In an instant, we're tangled in each other all over again. We spend the next hour indulging in every inch of each other. His mouth is on my neck. My hand is on the bulge in his pants that swells against my touch. We lose our clothes and then, we lose our minds. We don't stop until we're panting in each other's arms.

So much for keeping this uncomplicated.

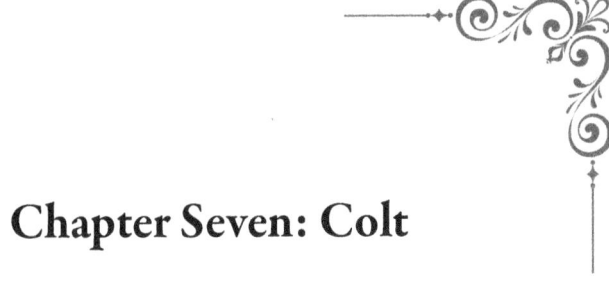

Chapter Seven: Colt

The last week with Hannah by my side has been a beautiful distraction from all the things I *should* be doing. I should be worrying about my future. Making investments with my money from the tour. Buying a proper family home. Considering my father's not-so-subtle offer to join the firm or at least the country club. I should be sleeping. Being present in any conversation. But None of it happens.

I can't focus for a minute on anything other than Hannah. She's beautiful in a way I've never experienced. Strong but fragile, independent but loyal. Hannah has filled my world with bright vibrant colors I'm seeing for the first time through her eyes. She's nothing like the women I've dated in the past and I have a feeling she's supposed to be my future.

"Hey, I was just thinking about you." I can't help the way my mouth curls up into a ridiculous smile when Hannah steps into the clubhouse. "How's the mural going?"

"Today's is right in the lobby of the hotel and it's getting pretty crowded over there so I'm taking a little break. Figured I'd head over to the best golf course in town and see if I could flirt with the staff." Hannah runs her finger across my chest and her touch sends goosebumps rippling across me.

"I guess it's my lucky day." I put a hand on her cheek and pull her in for a kiss.

When the door to the clubhouse opens behind us, Hannah pulls away from me.

"Son." My father's voice makes me bolt upright.

I forgot that he was heading in this morning to play a round of golf with the guys. I should have warned Hannah. It's too late for me, but she could have saved herself.

"Hey, Dad." I give him a nod as he barrels toward us, two equally stuffy friends in tow. "You remember Hannah from the Valentine's party?"

"Pleasure, how could I forget?" He holds out his hand to Hannah in a stiff, mildly off-putting gesture and she takes it with a smile. "Colt, Hank, and Thomas here were anxious to see you. They followed your progress on the tour. Made a little money betting on you over at the club."

"Thanks for the vote of confidence." I let out a chuckle. "Good to see you, gentlemen."

Hank steps forward. "How are you kid? When are you gonna come up and join the firm?"

"Ah, I see Dad has you doing his bidding. I work here now, running the course and the clubhouse. It may be a while before I flex my investment muscles." *Like forever. I can't think of a more drab existence.*

"Well, we've got a spot for you at the table for poker night too. Maybe we'll see you there," Hank says. His eyes dart to Hannah. "So, Hannah, what do you do?"

Her mouth pulls into a tight line. "I work here, painting murals. That's why I look like this." She gestures down at her paint-covered black shirt and does an adorable little curtsey. "But mostly, I'm a nanny for my sister and for Roman and Stella. Maybe you know them, they work here."

Thomas nudges me. "Ah, I see she's working on that M-R-S degree."

"M-R-S degree?" Hannah furrows her eyebrows, demanding clarification.

"Yeah, hey, I think it's great. A pretty girl like you, you spend enough time around the guys in the clubhouse and soon you won't have to work at all." Hank lets out a throaty chuckle and my father joins in the laughter.

"Hannah's an incredible artist. She painted that mural..." I start but my father and his friends aren't listening.

"Sure, sure." Dad holds up a hand, stopping me. "You know, Hannah, my wife hosts a ladies' tea on Sundays out at our home. You should come. I'm sure she'd love to get to know you. Maybe save the painted clothing though." He laughs.

"*Indoctrinate you* is more like it. That's enough," I snap. "That's good Dad, no one is joining the firm right now and I think Hannah is plenty set with things to do. Why don't you guys t-off?"

"That's my son for you, always the sensitive one." Dad nods to Thomas and Hank and it makes fury bubble within me.

I've had it. I hate being in these situations with my father and I'm sure as hell not going to put Hannah through them. I put a hand on Hannah's back and usher her away from the chaos. Though something tells me she'd fare better in these situations than I do.

When my father and his minions disappear, I search Hannah's face. I can't imagine what she's thinking. "Are you okay? I'm sorry about them. Once my father starts drinking, there's no telling what else will come out of his mouth. I'd like to not scare you off this soon. I just found you."

Her downturned mouth pulls up into a smile. "You're Dad is pretty intense."

"Yeah, he can be."

"I have to ask, are you on your way out of here to join the firm or the club or whatever he's got going on? He seems to think you are and I don't know if I can imagine a version of you in a white button-down handing out passive-aggressive comments to women." She bites her bottom lip.

"No, I'm not. I'm not crazy about the way they live. It's all very surface. There's a reason I've put it off for so long."

"Oh come on, they think you're a chip off the old block. Colt Calloway, the next member of... the firm." She wiggles her fingers ominously with a giggle.

"No actually. I'm not even from the same block. I'm adopted and I didn't know it." The words burn as they leave my throat. The pain of the realization is too new, too real. It's not something I planned on sharing, but somehow telling Hannah my truth feels right.

"Oh, I didn't know." She tucks a strand of hair behind her ear.

I continue, "In fact, I only just found out a few years ago when I finished my last pro tour and moved back here. I'm lucky to have been adopted as a baby by two people who wanted a child so badly. But they should have told me. Finding out as an adult was weird. All of a sudden I feel like I'm just this person floating through life, pretending to be a part of this family. I knew I didn't quite fit with them, but I chalked it up to the enormous generation gap. They are old parents, from another time, not willing to keep up with the ways of the world."

Hannah leans back against the bartop. Her face is thoughtful, head nodding, eyes wrinkled at the corners. "Do you know your birth parents or their story?"

"No. I've thought about it since the moment they told me I was adopted. I want to know my truth. A part of that truth is that I have two people who have loved me since birth and given their whole hearts to me. I feel selfish for thinking that it isn't enough. I want to know where I come from, but maybe in time..." I trail off. "You're lucky to have known your parents and you and your sister are so close. What's it like having a sibling like that? I always thought my life would have been better if I'd had a sibling."

"Yeah, my sister is incredible and we had amazing parents. We are lucky in that way. But we lost them when we were so young. My sister gave the best years of her life to raising me. She didn't have to, but I never heard her complain once. She's worked so hard and given me so much. That's why I feel so bad about the possibility of leaving for art school." Hannah crosses her arms over her chest. "Families... can't live with them, can't live without them." She shakes her head with a laugh.

"Your sister chose her path because she loves you. But you don't owe it to her to live the rest of your life doing what you think she wants you to do."

"That's funny, I was going to say the same thing to you about your parents." She raises an eyebrow at me.

"I do wonder who I would have been if I was never adopted. It's weird, right? Would you be sitting here with me if your parents hadn't passed away so long ago? Because I think we were meant to end up here right now like this, together. Me and you against everything." I take her hands in mine.

"Me and you." Hannah rises on her tiptoes and presses her forehead against mine. "For now."

I hold her there. To be understood like this, to be seen, it's intoxicating. When Hannah looks up at me, I plant my mouth on hers. This time our kiss is slow and careful. Her lips send tingles whipping up and down my spine that leave me breathless. Our tongues dance, pressing together and conveying everything that I can't find the words to say.

Somehow I know that this is just one kiss of a thousand more with this woman who has captured my whole heart like a thief in the night. When we finally pull away, she looks up at me. Her eyes sparkling in the reflection of the sunlight.

"You should come over for dinner with my family. It's nothing like the tea I've just been invited to, I can tell you that much. It'll just be my sister and Shawn, Roman will be there with Stella too. And of course the girls McKenna and Rosie. It's a fun group, casual and welcoming. I promise no one will ask you about your plans for the future or try to convince you to join any clubs. What do you think?"

"I can't say no to you, even if I wanted to... and I don't want to." I take her hand in mine. "I'll be there."

Chapter Eight: Hannah

H*i Hannah, this is Leon with the admissions department calling again. I just wanted to congratulate you on your acceptance into our program and make sure you don't have any questions. We know that you're facing a life-changing decision and if we can be of any assistance, don't hesitate to reach out. Otherwise, we look forward to receiving your response.*

The voicemail from the admission office plays over and over in my mind. I know I need to give them a decision about whether or not I'm planning to attend in the fall. Acceptance into an art school on the coast is exactly what I hoped for when I completed over a dozen application packets. But now that the time has come to commit, I can't bring myself to pull the trigger.

There's something about it that feels... off. I don't know whether I'll find my place in Misty Mountain, but something about life in the city doesn't feel right either. But right now, I can't think about any of that because we're gathered at my sister's house around her kitchen table and the whole gang is here.

Colt sits between Roman and me, across the table from Stella and Shawn. My sister Kaylee is currently running back and forth from the kitchen bringing out countless trays of dessert and refusing to let anyone help her. And the girls, McKenna and Rosie sit at the end of the table, grinning ear to ear and whispering to each other conspiratorily.

The meal has gone surprisingly well. Colt seems to be making a good impression on everyone in the room. I like the feeling of having him beside me even if I have been a little distracted by my impending decision.

Ding. Ding.

Shawn taps the side of his glass with his knife.

"What are you doing?" Kaylee lets out a laugh.

"I'd like to make a toast. To friends old and new, and to Colt. Thanks for coming tonight. We're so happy that Hannah has brought you into our world. Cheers." Shawn raises his glass.

"Cheers!" Rosie squeals from the end of the table.

"Thanks for having me. It's nice to be at a normal, non-stuffy dinner party. Roman has been raving about this little group and I can see why." Colt takes a sip of his drink and Roman nods.

As I look around the table, I try to imagine that this could be my every Sunday night for the rest of my life. It isn't terrible. All of us gathered. There is a charm to it. I like the way Colt fits in with my family already. It's fun and warm.

As the dessert brigade continues, my sister breaks out the board games. For once, I have a built-in teammate. These are the people I love most in this world and I can picture Colt being a part of this. Still, my mind wanders.

It isn't ever going to get any better than Colt, that's obvious. But is this how it's supposed to be? Is this the whole picture for my life? Or is there more?

Buzz. Buzz.

My phone vibrates against the wood table. I glance at it and wince when I see the words, *admission office,* glowing on the screen. I flip it face down.

"What was that?" Colt leans over, whispering into my ear.

"Nothing, I don't want to talk about it right now." I tuck a strand of hair behind my ear.

"You're not going are you?" There's a panic in Colt's whisper. "Tell them to stop calling."

My eyes dart around the room. The last thing I need right now is to drum up any suspicion about my future in front of my sister and Stella. Panic over childcare will not be helpful in this situation.

"No. I'm not." I brush him off and shake my head though he doesn't seem to understand the magnitude of the conversation he's trying to bring up so casually.

"What's wrong?" Kaylee's eyes burn into mine and she pauses the game.

"Nothing. We're good." My heart rate ticks up. *I can't handle this right now.*

The thought of leaving my sister and Colt has every muscle in me clenching with discomfort. The effect on Colt seems to be the same. I don't even want to think about how this conversation would end if I enlightened Kaylee right now.

Would she cry? Be frustrated? Think that I'm ungrateful? And what about Colt? Would he move on immediately? But are my dreams not worth the discomfort? I take a sip of my wine. No matter my decision, now is certainly not the time to talk about it.

Colt fidgets in his seat, sitting on his hands and nearly spilling his glass of red wine.

I cut my eyes at him. "Are you good?"

"Yes. More than good actually. I'm the best I've been in a long while and I'm excited too. I have an announcement." Colt talks louder than necessary.

"An announcement?" *What the hell is this?*

He clears his throat and taps his glass with his knife in the same way Shawn had only moments earlier. When the chatter at the table falls silent and all eyes are on him, Colt gives a smile that is a weird mix of grimace and nerves.

He gets to his feet, his chair making a loud screeching sound across my sister's floor. "Hannah," Colt says my name like a declaration and then clears his throat again. "Hannah, I think we should get married.

I don't have a diamond ring with me, this is sort of a last-minute decision. But my parents will surely be happy and I'll get you as big a ring as you want."

The room falls silent. My mouth falls open in pure terror.

"Yep. So, we can do this." Colt compensates for my lack of enthusiasm by laying it on thick and I think I might be sick.

"What?" My sister's voice floats above the sound of my heart pounding in my chest. There's a hint of amusement in the way it turns up at the end, puncturing the shock in the room.

"Can I be a flower girl?" Rosie chimes in.

"Me too!" Mckenna adds.

"No," I shake my head at the girls.

"No?" Shawn asks. "You won't have the girls in the wedding?"

"Stop! No, they could be in the wedding, if there was a wedding, but there isn't. There's no wedding to be in." My words come out in a jumbled mess. "No one is getting married right now." "What are you doing Colt?"

"I'm proposing!" He holds his hands out to me as if I'm missing the point.

My head spins. "You *think* you want to marry me because it would make your parents happy?" I press a hand to my forehead. I can't believe this.

Colt's eyes whip around all the faces at the table. There are silent, horrified stares all around us. I shake my head.

Colt pulls his shoulders back and stands up tall. "Well, I don't want you to leave for art school. The coast is far and overrated. I'm not stupid, I know my time to convince you to stay is running out. If I didn't propose, you'd accept the admissions offer and I'd miss my chance. Hell, you may even accept it still. I saw the look on your face when you talked about getting out of this town. It broke my heart and I'm doing my part for all of us at this table to keep you here."

"What?" This time, Kaylee's voice is shrill. The edge of amusement in her tone is gone. "What's he talking about?"

Oh shit.

"I'm not going." I look at my sister.

"Going where?" Kaylee demands.

"Great!" Colt gets to one knee and takes my hand in his. "So you aren't going. We're getting married."

"You're getting married? For reals this time? Because I want to be a flower girl." McKenna shrieks, her hands balled with excitement.

"Colt, get up." My words slip out through clenched teeth and I lower my voice. "In what world does a half-hearted proposal in front of my whole family make this better?" I swallow back my tears. "I can't do this right now."

"But you're it for me, I know that. I've never been so happy," Colt says.

A hot knot tightens over my chest making it hard to breathe. There isn't any air left in this room and I need to leave.

"Excuse me." I dash the front door.

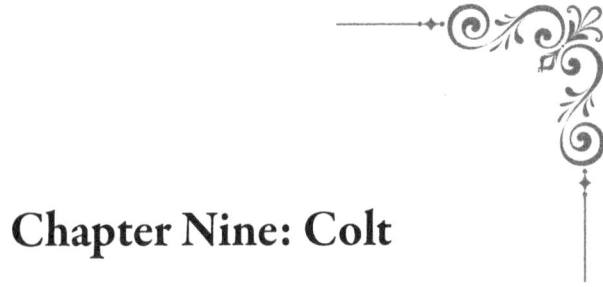

Chapter Nine: Colt

"I'm sorry. Hannah... shit. I didn't think it was going to be like that. In my mind, it was so much better. I'm sorry. I figured you already told her. You tell your sister everything. How was I supposed to know? Stop walking!" I follow her out through the front door as she darts toward her car. My heart pounds in my chest. I feel dizzy, scrambling, desperate to find the words to fix this.

When she has one hand on the door handle of her car, Hannah's pace slows for the first time. She folds her arms across her stomach and hesitates.

"Can we just talk about this? Please?" I catch up with her and put a hand low on her back.

When she turns, Hannah's face is pinched into tight lines. But she doesn't look angry, she looks... sad. Her eyes are glassy. Her mouth turns down at the corners.

"I'm sorry. That was a terrible, half-hearted proposal and it should have never happened. I embarrassed both of us in front of your family. I told you that I only think we should get married. That wasn't it. It wasn't right." I take her hand in mine and she doesn't pull away. For a moment, it seems like we may be able to get past this and it's all I want to do. My stomach trembles.

Hannah swallows hard and looks up at me from beneath her long, dark, lashes. "Colt, why do you want to marry me?"

I blink back my surprise at her question. That's the last thing I expected her to ask. I'm flustered all over again.

"Well... because I don't want you to leave. I've fallen in love with you. Because it's what I should be doing. My dad's right, I'm thirty-three, there isn't any reason I shouldn't settle and make a life here. I want that to be with you." My sentences come out in a messed-up jumble. I know the words are all wrong the moment they pass through my lips.

She shakes her head. "That isn't a reason. It doesn't even sound like you. It sounds like you want to live up to your family's expectations of the man they think you are. I can understand that, I really can. But it isn't the real you and it definitely isn't the real me. I won't choose a life based on anyone else's expectations."

"Let's figure this out together." I swallow the lump in my throat. "It doesn't have to be here. We can move if that's what you want."

"It isn't the place, Colt. I may very well end up here at the end of the day. But it'll be on my own terms. You should try it. Live on your own terms. Figure out who you are and what you want for yourself, not for anyone else." Hannah's lips are pressed into a thin line as she takes a step away from me.

Her words burn in my chest. I'm losing her, and there's nothing I can do to stop it. After all, she's right. I have no idea who I am. I don't even know where I come from. There are so many pieces I haven't figured out but I'm sure about her. I want to tell her that, but every time I open my mouth I only seem to dig my hole deeper.

Hannah opens the door and climbs into the front seat of her car. "I need to go."

"Where are you going?"

"I'm going to work on figuring out what will make me happy. I need adventures. If I'm ever going to choose this place, I need to know what the other options are and I think you should do the same." She leans into her car, then turns back to me. "If you decide to stay here and find someone to marry, she'll be the luckiest girl in the world and I mean that. But it can't be me, it isn't fair to either one of us."

Hannah puts her key in the ignition and I feel completely lost. I've never been more sure about anything in my life. I love Hannah and I love who I am when I'm with Hannah. *How the hell did I mess this up so badly?*

Right now, there's nothing left to say because I can tell she's done listening. So I blow out a deep breath and take a step away from her car before spouting out one more lie. "It's okay, I'll give you all the time you need."

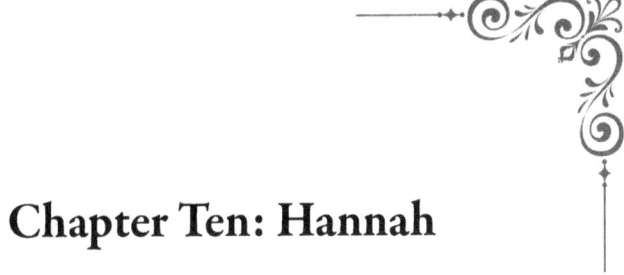

Chapter Ten: Hannah

Rosie and McKenna giggle from inside the fort they've built in my living room. Normally I'd climb in right beside them, but I don't have it in me today.

It's been three days without Colt and they are darker than I expected. I knew better than to think that someone could love me without changing me. It happens every single time. I'm sure that not every man is like this, but the ones I pick sure are.

At the first opportunity, Colt asked me to give up my dreams in pursuit, not of his own, but of the life his parents want for him. As I replay the scene at the dinner table, it makes nausea swirl in my stomach. I let my guard down and here I am again, alone and totally devastated.

The sound of tires pulling into my driveway has me glancing out of my tiny kitchen window. A part of me hopes it's Colt, but at the same time, I need it to not be Colt. My breath catches in my throat and I don't exhale fully until I see that it's only my sister coming to pick up my niece.

"Rosie, your Mom's here honey. Put your shoes on."

In the last few days, my sister has given me the space I desperately need. She's good like that. But the awkwardness between us at the dinner table hasn't passed, it's only been pushed to the side. I know we need to talk about this at some point, but I dread the conversation and I hope to buy myself a little more time.

But from the way my sister opens my front door and plops into a chair at my kitchen table, I think the moment has arrived. *Ready or not, here we go.*

"Mom, no! I don't want to leave yet." Rosie shouts from inside the pillow fort.

"Hi to you too," Kaylee laughs. "You can have a few minutes. I need to talk to Aunt Hannah."

My stomach flips on itself. As hard as we work at it, the relationship between my sister and me always teeters more on parent-child than true siblings. It's a by-product of the way we grew up and it doesn't make talks like this any easier.

Kaylee turns to me. "Hey, I've been trying to give you some space but we need to talk and just get back to normal already. Don't you agree?"

"Yeah, of course, I do." I brace myself for the hard conversation I know is coming, shaking my nerves out of my hands. "I'm sorry that I didn't tell you about art school. It's not even something I know for sure I want to do, but I want the option. You've given up so much for me, taken care of me when you didn't have to. Your life has been about sacrifice. Helping you raise Rosie is the least I can do. Besides, she's my niece. I love her as if she were my own kid..." I trail off.

I can hardly look at my sister. The last thing I want to do is hurt her, but I can tell by the way my words bring a sense of relief in my chest that this conversation is long overdue. When I finally look up, Kaylee doesn't look upset at all. In fact, her mouth is curled up into a smile and I am totally confused.

"I'm the one who's sorry. I put so much pressure on you to come to Misty Mountain with Rosie and me. I couldn't imagine our lives without you. But just because something is right for me doesn't mean it's right for you." She gets up and puts a kettle on the stove.

"I don't hate this town, it's charming and picturesque. But I am struggling to find my place here. And I wouldn't want to miss time with Rosie. Not for the world. So my plan is only half-baked."

Kaylee shakes her head as she gets two mugs from the cabinet. "Listen to me, there was a time in my life when I couldn't have done it without you. You've never owed me anything and I'm so grateful for the years you spent helping me raise her. Having a child was my choice. As hard as it's been at times, it's what I wanted for my life and I'm so happy."

"I love how close I get to be to my niece. If I left—" I start, but Kaylee stops me.

"I know and she loves you the most. But I'm settled here with Shawn and I can promise you that I'm not going anywhere. You should live for *yourself*. Take your time. Explore. Go to art school... or don't. You don't owe me anything and I'll be here cheering you on every step of the way."

I let out a deep exhale. I don't give my sister enough credit. She comes through for me time and time again and I always worry. As much as I don't want to admit it, I needed my sister to say that. I needed to hear that she is okay. That she *wants* me to chase my dreams. I feel lighter. I feel like anything is possible.

Tears of relief seep from the corners of my eyes. "Thank you, I don't think I realized how much I needed to hear that."

"Hey, you never have anything to worry about with me. I'd support you in anything you wanted to do. I hope you know that. If it's art school, I'll help you find a way to pay. If it's a job on the coast somewhere, I'll come to visit."

"What will you do about a nanny? And Stella too? I can't imagine sending these two to a daycare." I wince at the thought of my niece in some sterile institution of a daycare.

"Well, with baby number two on the way, Shawn and I were thinking it may be for the best if I stay home for a few years. So there won't be a problem. Just promise me that I can come to visit you from time to time, you know when I'm ready to tear my hair out." Kaylee giggles as she pats her belly.

"I don't know where I'll be, but I'll always have space for you. And a drink waiting," I say.

"I'm there! For now, your only job is to find out what you want to do, where you want to do it... and who you want to do it with." Kaylee smirks at me over her mug of tea.

"Stop it," I laugh.

"But seriously, What are you going to do about Colt?" Kaylee asks the other question I've been avoiding.

"No idea." I shake my head. I miss him terribly.

I sip my tea too. Having this conversation with my sister has freed up space in my mind to think through the situation with Colt. I like him, more than I should. More than I care to admit. I might even be in love with him. He's charming and protective. He makes me laugh.

But I can't marry him right now and if that's the path he's on, I don't want to keep him from finding someone who wants the same things he does. The thought is crushing. I don't want to lose him, but right now, I can't see any other way.

"What do you want to do about Colt?"

What do I want to do? Hug him. Fall into his arms. Take his clothes off. Talk to him until the early hours of the morning. Stay glued to his side. Tell him all my secrets.

But as my sister's stare meets mine, all I can get out is, "I want to think on it."

Chapter Eleven: Colt

It's been nearly a week since the dinner party heard round the world and I'm at a complete loss as to how to fix it. The last few days have been quiet, too quiet. Now I'm at work making my best attempt at carrying on, but Roman knows something is still off with me. He's done me the solid of not making me relive my terrible proposal, but it's the elephant in the room for sure.

"What? Just say it already." I look at him from across the clubhouse.

"Okay. That was a mess the other night, bro. A total mess. You told her you wanted to marry her because your father wants you to. I've had some bad dates but that was one for the books. What were you thinking?"

Hearing Roman say the words aloud releases the tension in my chest. It's like I've been holding my breath and he's finally let the air out. I don't like what he's saying, but I know the truth when I hear it and I have to let out a laugh.

"I don't know. I thought that's what she wanted. Only, I didn't. She told me she wanted to leave, explore, maybe go to art school. I just thought I was giving her a reason to stay, I guess."

"But you don't even know if staying here is what you want. All I've heard from you in the last year is that you don't know what to do with yourself now that your golf career is over. You don't feel like you fit in with your family. You wonder if there's more for you than this town." Roman tilts his head to the side like I might be crazy.

Maybe I am. Maybe I'm so crazy about Hannah that it has me acting out of desperation. But that isn't a good look. Now that I've had time to see more clearly, a proposal is probably the last thing she wanted. I may be confused about a lot of things in my life, but one thing is for certain.

"I want her. I'm falling for her faster than I know how to handle it." I shake my head. *What the hell is happening to me?*

"I get it, I do, but you need to figure out your own shit first. I'm only telling you this because we're friends. You need to put in the work. Taking the time to become the man you want to be and all that good shit." He lets out a chuckle and gets back to work, securing the loose shelf behind the bar.

"I don't want to lose her in the meantime. There's no doubt there, I want her in my world. But I want her to chase her dreams, but I want to be a part of that. I don't want to be left behind. I'm not an anchor, I can help her get to where she's going."

Roman pauses, looking up at me. "So that's what you say, man. That right there. None of this, my parents think I should settle down bullshit. Next time you get the chance, that's what you say to her."

"If there is a next time." I feel the muscles in my throat tighten.

Roman puts his drill down on the bartop and turns to face me. "Listen, I get it. I was there at dinner, and even though I didn't see much of you that night, believe me, I'll never forget it." He raises a teasing eyebrow at me. "But Hannah is a good person. Talk to her. I think you'll be surprised how understanding she is. I've seen her bend over backward for the people she loves, her sister, Stella, and the girls. I think she'd probably put you in that category."

As he talks, I think of all the ways Hannah has inadvertently made me fall in love with her. Her creativity, beauty, sex appeal, her enormous heart. The truth is, I don't know if I can fix this. But what I do know is that I don't want to be without her.

Roman continues, "Give her some credit. If you're sure about her, take action. Make sure you have a chance to say your piece."

By the time he finishes talking, I'm already digging my phone out of my pocket. "I'm way ahead of you. I have something in mind. But it's going to take a little more than a conversation."

"That's right, don't take no for an answer. How can I help?" Roman asks.

The next hours pass in a whirlwind of chaos. In the end, it comes down to three hours of research. Two bags of snacks from the grocery store. And one text message asking her to meet me outside of her house. My heart pounds in my chest. No matter what her reply is I know that nothing will ever be the same.

Chapter Twelve: Hannah

When the text message from Colt comes through, butterflies flutter in my stomach, even though I wish they wouldn't. If I'm ever going to get over Colt, I can't throw away my resolve every time he contacts me. But that's exactly what I want to do. My stream of thoughts bubbles up the way it has for the last few days.

Maybe I should have said yes. Maybe marrying Colt would change my life in a million beautiful ways. So what if it was his parent's idea. But then... It was his parent's idea. Who marries someone who only thinks they want to marry you?

I clear all of the clutter from my mind and reply with a simple, yes I will meet you outside. Now I'm standing on my own porch with my hands on my hips and my heart on my sleeve waiting for his big truck to pull into my small driveway.

When his loud engine finally rumbles up the road, Colt parks quickly and hops out. He looks as handsome as ever in his casual black hoodie and dark pants. He's holding a brown grocery bag in one hand as he bounds toward me.

"Hannah, thanks for meeting me. I'm sorry about the other night. I fucked up, big time. I want to make things right with you." He puts his arms around me, pulls me in for a tight hug, and then takes a half step back. "I came to give you this."

I squint my eyes at Colt, trying to make sense of his rambling. He holds out his truck keys to me and then the brown grocery bag. When I peer inside the bag, it's filled with food and I am filled with confusion.

"Keys? You came here to give me keys to your truck?" There's a legit chance that he's lost his mind. "I have a car."

"Not only keys... keys and snacks." Colt holds out an overflowing bag of groceries and his mouth curls up into a smile on one side.

"Your look says it's all settled and believe me, I wish that were the case. I love to eat my feelings as much as the next girl but seriously, a bag of chips and a pack of gummy bears isn't going to fix this." I press my fingertips to my temples.

"But it *is* settled." Colt looks totally unphased and if he's found a solution, I wish he'd share the good news with me already.

"Colt, I like you, I'm falling for you faster than I know how to handle. But at the end of the day, nothing's changed. I don't know if I can be in Misty Mountain. I might be okay here, but I haven't lived enough to know for sure. And you have so many things to work through with your family. You want to find your birth parents. You don't like golf anymore. Sweetheart, you don't know who you are. We aren't ready for love. We need to figure ourselves out first." My words catch in my chest. I don't like the reality I'm laying out for him but I know it's the truth. "I only want to get married one time so I won't let us bypass all the individual learning we need to do before we make that commitment. I'm trying to be responsible about this, take it slow for once."

"You're right." He nods. "Listen, I want to marry you. I don't apologize for that and my offer won't expire. I'm not here to convince you to push everything you want aside and settle down with me. That's what my parents want. Even though I have some work to do in finding out who I am, I know I'm not them. I knew I loved you the moment I saw you in your ball gown covered in paint. But I'm okay with us ending up together being down the line. You can take your time getting there because I trust you will. When you're ready, I'll be right here."

"Thank you." For a moment, his words suck the panic right out of me. I'm surrounded by overwhelming calm. But then something prickles on the back of my neck. "But what if I'm not here. What if my searching takes me beyond Misty Mountain to some art school in a big city. I don't want you to wait for me." The words hurt as they leave my throat.

Colt shakes his head and his mouth pulls up at the corner. "Sweetheart, I'm going with you. I need to find myself as much as you do. Away from golf and away from Misty Mountain. I need to breathe, collect the pieces of my past so that I can choose my own future."

"What are you thinking? Could you really leave this place where your roots run so deep? Is it in you? And what would your parents say?" My heart rate ticks up and cautious optimism washes over me.

Colt steps closer to me and slides a hand over my shoulder. Then pulls out his phone. "I've mapped it all out. We're going on an epic road trip. We're gonna see every museum, every piece of street art, and all the things in between. We're gonna take our time. I've already talked to your sister and Stella too. They want you to go, they'll work out the babysitting between them while we're gone." The muscles in Colt's throat clench. "And if you're up for it... We're going to find my birth mother. I'd like you by my side when I meet her."

My mouth falls open. "You're kidding. This is exactly what I need. But you're sure you want to do this? All of it... and with me? I don't do things that are normal."

"I'm counting on it." He plants a kiss on my cheek. "I want to be the man in your world. In order to do that, I have to know who I am. So I say we take the time to find ourselves, together... and just so you know, you deserve *all* the adventures. You aren't your sister. Her life has turned out exactly as it was supposed to. I've seen the way she looks at Shawn, they're happy. Fair or not, you have more choices than she did. It isn't your fault that her life was hard and I'd guess that she is more than happy with how it's all turned out. Right now, I'm not asking you to make a lifelong decision. All I'm asking is that you choose me. Come with me on an adventure of a lifetime. I promise you Misty Mountain will be here when we get back, *if* we come back. There aren't any rules here."

Tears fill my eyes. "How can you be real? This is a perfect solution. But I can't afford it."

"So I will, I can't think of a better way to spend my money from the tour." He shrugs.

With all my concerns resolved in Colt's capable hands, I can't say yes fast enough. My heart swells and warmth flutters through me.

"I want to find myself with you." A calm settles over me. "I want to live my life for me and somehow I know you are going to be a big part of that."

"I promise you that I will never stop you from becoming the person you are meant to be. All I ask is to stand by your side on your way there." Colt wraps his arms around me. "It's you and me, babe. It'll always be me and you, no matter where we are."

Chapter Thirteen: Colt

Three Months Later

Life on the road with Hannah in the last few months has been a whirlwind of bliss. We've driven up and down the coast, slept under the stars, and visited every piece of art I could find for her along the way.

I've fallen in love with every ounce of her. Her wild hair. Her easy smile. Hannah makes my world go round. She's herself in every situation and she's encouraged me to find myself too. That's exactly what I'm doing today.

The early summer sun casts a golden glow over Hannah as she stands by my side on the front porch of the tiny brick house. This trip has been a long time coming. Now that this moment is finally here, it's surreal. There's an electric charge in the air, the warm summer air crackles with the promise of resolutions long overdue.

"This is it, I guess. All the answers I've always needed. Or maybe at least a place to start. All I have to do is knock." My stomach twists and turns, tying itself into knots. The anticipation makes me sick.

"Hey, look at me." Hannah intertwines her fingers with mine and it overwhelms me with comfort. "No matter what happens you'll have more information than you do right now. That's a good thing. But no matter what happens, none of it changes the fact that you are an amazing man. It has nothing to do with golf, either." She gives me an encouraging nod. "You can do this."

Hannah's unwavering support makes me want to cry. I don't know what I did in this lifetime to deserve such an incredible woman standing by my side. But I'm grateful.

I shift my weight between my feet and widen my stance, trying to stabilize myself. "Thank you, sweetheart. Here goes nothing." I take another deep breath and bring my hand to the door.

Knock. Knock.

The door opens slowly and a woman with my eyes stares back at me. "Colt." Her voice is soft and my name on her lips is strange and foreign. She's an odd combination of young and weary. She can't be more than fifteen years older than me. The lines and wrinkles around her eyes are too deep with too many stories to tell for someone so young.

As the woman stares at me, Hannah presses her palm to mine, running her thumb across the back of my hand. My heart pounds out of my chest.

The woman nods. Tears well in the corners of her eyes. "My son."

I'm in a state of shock. The world seems to spin and I cement my feet to the ground in an attempt to stay upright. Then, Hannah lets go of my hand and places it on my back. One gentle push from her propels me forward.

My birth mother opens her arms to me and I sink into them. "Mom."

"Colt, I've hoped for this day all my life. I was young, but I've always loved you. Always. I can't believe you're here."

Tears stream down my face as my birth mother wraps her thin arms around me. I feel something change deep within me. *The missing parts of myself weren't me at all, they were all her. My birth mother. I'm so glad I'm here and I would have never come if it weren't for Hannah.*

Being present in this moment is a heartstopping collision of past and future. I feel a flash of hope course through me. In her eyes, I see a glimpse of the man I was meant to be and the life I could have had. My birth mother, the missing piece to the puzzle of my past is here. It's all thanks to Hannah, the key to my future.

"Come in, please, we have so much to talk about..."

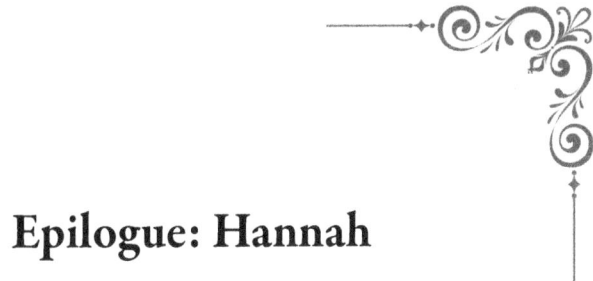

Epilogue: Hannah

One Year Later

    With Colt by my side, everything seems so clear. I was always meant to end up in Misty Mountain. I have the career I've always dreamed of, working full time as a mural artist at Brew by Brewer. It took me leaving to realize it. But more importantly, we're living our own lives with our friends and family by our sides.

After that first visit, Colt has kept in touch with his birth mother. Knowing where he comes from has allowed him to grow into a man who is confident in where he's heading. And where he's heading is straight into my arms.

Colt and I moved in together right away. Now every day feels like an adventure. It's blissfully simple and completely us. But still, I can't help the way my heart pounds in my chest when I imagine the look on Colt's face when I tell him the news later today.

I step out of the shower and wrap myself in a towel. I pace back and forth, waiting for Colt to get home. The minutes seem to stretch on for hours. Finally, I hear the door and my rock up on my toes, giddy with excitement.

"Whew, if it isn't the sexiest woman in the world." Colt's voice wraps around me like a warm hug. He puts his arms around my waist from behind. "I like the look, you should wear this all the time." He nuzzles against the back of my hair.

I lean into his embrace and my heart flutters as I nestle into him. If he only knew what he was in for, I shake my nerves out of my fingertips.

"What are you up to, I've been wanting you to come for the last hour or so. I need to talk to you about something important."

"Well, that works out because I was out on a top-secret mission. I need to talk to you about something important too," he says.

I turn to face him. "Mine is pretty important," I mumble under my breath.

He continues. "I thought long and hard about how I wanted to do this. Whether I needed flowers or chocolates or candles. But at the end of the day, those things aren't us. This right here, this is us. Me and you standing side by side and hand in hand. Marching off rhythm to the beat of our own drum. Making promises. Making art. Making love." Colt reaches into his pocket.

I gasp at the sight of a gold ring with a bright blue sapphire in the center. "This *is* important."

"Yeah, it's the most important." He laughs and then drops to one knee. "I figured you wouldn't want anything traditional and this one felt like you. Hannah Allen, you've painted the color back into my world. You've taught me to find myself. I love every part of you and I want to keep you all for myself. I want to walk this life by your side, hand in hand. Will you marry me?"

I can't talk over the sound of my heart pounding in my chest. Colt is nothing if not consistent, unknowingly perfect in his timing. The tears that have brimmed behind my eyes all day spill from the corners and I nod my head.

"Yes? Is that a yes?" His mouth curls up into a smile.

"Yes." I manage to choke out my words, but just barely.

Colt lets out a heavy breath as he slides the ring onto my finger and I try to swallow the lump in my throat. When he gets back to his feet, an uncontrollable sob escapes from deep within me. I put my face in my hands.

Since the moment I took the test, my emotions have been all over the place. But now, all of my worries. My doubt. My fear. It's all gone. There isn't anything left but pure unadulterated joy.

"Hey, are you okay? This is supposed to be a happy occasion," Colt chuckles as he runs a hand down the length of my back. "It's me and you from here on out."

"I am happy. This is especially good timing." I look up at him through tear-stained eyes.

"Thank you, I tried. I figured that everything is better when you're naked."

I shake my head with a laugh. "No, you don't get it. I was going to surprise you today." I inhale a deep breath through my nose. "It isn't only you and me from here on out. It can't be. Colt, I'm pregnant."

His mouth falls open and Colt's expression goes blank. He looks at me, blinking, mouth open. "And now it's my turn to cry." His voice is a whisper. "I can't believe it. I'm going to have a person who is half me. I've never known anyone who shares my blood before. A family. My own family."

"Yes, our own little family." The knot on my chest loosens.

"This is too good to be true. Are you sure? Why didn't you tell me?" He holds me away from him then drops a hand to my stomach.

"I wasn't keeping it from you. I only just found out. I wanted to confirm it with a doctor before I said anything. I didn't want to turn our world upside down unnecessarily. But I'm telling you now. She's twelve weeks old in there." My heart flutters in my chest. I already know this baby will have the best, most adoring dad.

"She?" His voice breaks.

I let out a giggle. "It's just a guess. But can't you imagine it? A sweet girl with her big, strong dad wrapped around her little finger. Rosie and McKenna settling right in with her. I can feel it and I'm so excited about it."

"A little artist who looks just like her mom." He rubs his hand back and forth across my stomach. "I'm going to have someone who shares my bloodline. She's going to be half me and there isn't anything that can ever take that away. And I get to share her with you." Tears spill down his cheeks. "This is the greatest gift of my life."

Colt holds me there for a good, long while. We spend the time dreaming up one million versions of happily ever after for our party of three. We make a list of all the people we want to tell and arrange to meet them in person with the news of our exciting announcement. My sister. His parents. Roman and Stella. The list of people who will be over the moon about this baby stretches to every part of Misty Mountain and beyond.

But in the end, we keep the news to ourselves for the night. We don't go anywhere. Instead, I fall asleep that night wrapped in Colt's arms wearing nothing but my ring. If there was any doubt in my mind about how Colt would handle the news of my pregnancy, it's long gone. I will spend every night, right here in his arms living my own happily ever after.

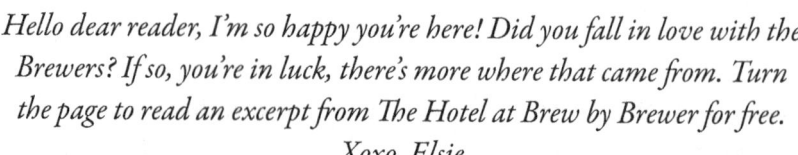

Hello dear reader, I'm so happy you're here! Did you fall in love with the Brewers? If so, you're in luck, there's more where that came from. Turn the page to read an excerpt from The Hotel at Brew by Brewer for free.
Xoxo, Elsie

THE HOTEL AT BREW BY Brewer, Book One Bellhop

Chapter One: Emery

"Hi." I keep my voice low as I sandwich my phone in the crook of my neck. "What's up Rick? I'm at work."

"Yeah, right, whatever. Listen, some of the guys I work with are heading over to watch the game so I need to drop off Miles early." My ex-husband's voice is flat and agitated.

"How early? I don't get off until six tonight." I peer out of my office at the line of guests forming in the lobby and waiting to check into our hotel. I'm a sales manager but at The Hotel at Brew by Brewer, we all pitch in anywhere we can. I should be out there helping.

"We're already in the car, about ten minutes away. I'm just going to have to leave him with you at work. Isn't there something he can do? Can't he just roam the property around the hotel for a few hours or play with that big dog that's always running around?"

I roll my eyes. This is just like Rick. "Are you kidding me, he's only eight. No he cannot roam—" I say, anger tightens in a knot on my chest making it harder to breathe.

"Hi Mom," my son Miles' voice comes on the line. I exhale and let my shoulders fall forward. "We're in the car. Dad said to tell you he can't come in when we get to your work because he doesn't have time. He said he'll just drop me in front of the hotel and you can meet me at the front desk."

I sigh. "It's all right bud, I'll be out front waiting for you. Just have your dad text me when you arrive."

"You got it bro! Just kidding Mom, you got it, Mom." Miles lets out a giggle.

When Miles hangs up I press my fingertips to my temples. Co-parenting with Rick is a nightmare, but at least I'm not his wife anymore, I have that going for me. I look back at the front desk and find my boss Jackson Brewer has beat me to helping and the line is already dwindling. So I take the opportunity to scroll through and respond to the dozens of emails waiting for me.

The Brew by Brewer property is a huge resort given the size of our tiny mountain town and there's never a dull moment. But today is especially hectic because not only are we down six people tonight, but the hotel is at full capacity. This isn't turning out to be quite the birthday I planned on. Not that I planned a wild party, but I could use a peaceful night floating in a bubble bath right about now.

Tap. Tap. Tap.

My door pushes open and Ellie, one of our event planners, steps inside and shuts the door behind her. "Happy birthday!" She holds up a cupcake from the cat cafe on our property with a single candle in it and a pack of matchsticks tucked beside it.

"You brought the one with the beer frosting, my favorite. Thank you!"

Ellie's sweet gesture makes me smile, especially because I know how busy she is right now since the hotel is hosting our twenty year high school reunion in just a week. She plops into the chair across from me and I reach for the cupcake, but she pulls it back with a shake of her head.

"Not a chance. We're going to do this the right way." Ellie strikes a match on the back of the matchbook and it sparks.

My eyes go wide. I bolt to my feet, lean over my desk, and blow the candle out with a laugh. "What are you, crazy? You can't light that in here, but really, thank you, it's so thoughtful."

"Fine, we'll have to pick a day you don't have Miles so I can drag you out to celebrate." Ellie sits back in her chair and I smirk at her. "Anyway, I was surprised to see the line in the lobby. Do you think people are already arriving for the reunion?"

"It seems like it's too soon, but I don't know. I've been making a point to keep my head down. It seems impossible that a full twenty years have gone by since we graduated. I don't want to see anyone from high school any more than I already do." Everyone in Misty Mountain was privy to the details of Rick's affair and the decline of my marriage three years ago. The thought still makes me uncomfortable.

"I mean, if I went, what would I say? You know that loser I dated in high school? Well if you haven't heard, I married him. He cheated on me. We had a kid. Our kid is amazing and Rick's still an asshole. So we're divorced," I laugh.

"And then you let your friend take you out for drinks and start dating again so you can find a real happily ever after... right? Who knows, maybe if you go you'll meet someone at the reunion," Ellie says.

"Uh, I already married someone from high school once, I don't know if that's the road I should head back down."

Ellie gives me a mischievous grin. "Speaking of high school, I stumbled across this gem in my reunion prep."

Ellie pulls a photo from her bag and holds it up. It's Rick and I at our senior homecoming and it makes me cringe. We're arm in arm standing in our king and queen crowns with homecoming-court sashes. Rick looks intoxicated from drinking the booze he stole from his parent's liquor cabinet before we left, a glaring red flag I ignored at the time.

I'm sober and despite having argued with Rick in the limo on the way to the dance, I'm beaming from ear to ear like a fool. My red hair is twisted back into curls secured by tiny clips shaped like butterflies. I used a Sharpie to write the words, *Nsync for life* on my wrist like a tattoo. I topped my look with a solid foundation a shade lighter than my already ghost pale skin tone and a truckload of body glitter on my overflowing cleavage. God bless the early two-thousands.

I thought I had it all figured out back then. Of course, I wouldn't actually change anything about my life even if I had the chance because my son came out of this beautiful disaster. But looking at my eighteen-year-old self now, I wish I could tell her to run. To leave this town and find more. To chase her dreams of going to art school.

But that was back when Rick was charming and I couldn't stop him from following me around like a puppy dog. I was naive and he was complex and exciting. I didn't stand a chance. Now I have to beg him to pick up his son every other weekend. Nausea rumbles deep in my stomach.

I take the photo from Ellie and slide it to the side of my desk. "Ugh, I don't want to look at that right now. Awful pictures aside, how's the reunion planning going?"

Creak.

"Mom?" My office door pushes open and Miles sticks his red tousled-haired head inside. He gives me a gap-toothed smile that melts my heart.

"Hey, bud." I stand and pull him into a tight hug. "I told your dad to text me, I would've met you out front." I'll never understand where Rick's head is at when it comes to making choices about our son.

"Hey Miles, my main man! I'm glad you're here to help. What are you going to be doing today? Checking people in?" Ellie puts her hand up and Miles gives her an enthusiastic high-five.

"I'm booked. I'm probably gonna get a ride in the elevator and push all the buttons," he lets out a wild giggle.

"Negative, mister." I bite back a smile. "You're going to be hanging out back here in my office. You can draw or play a game on my phone." My hope of getting through all my emails diminishes.

"Okay, I'll make something." Miles buzzes through my office opening drawers and gathering office supplies. "Wait, is that you and

Dad? Why do you have a crown? Why does Dad have that cape thing?" Miles holds up the dreadful homecoming picture and his mouth drops open.

"Yes, that was us back in high school. Let's put that away for now." I shoot Ellie a look and her mouth pulls into a grimace as she shrugs.

"No! I want to use it to make my Art-bot. He's a robot stuck in the web of tape." Miles tacks the photo to my corkboard.

"Actually, I was just ready to head back to my office. But Miles, I'll come to check on you in a little bit. I have a box of decorations to unpack. Maybe you can help me if it's okay with your mom," Ellie says.

"Can I?" Miles' eyebrows shoot up.

"Yes, let's let Ellie work for now and she'll come to get you when she's ready."

An hour passes and I fly through as many emails as I can. I schedule group packages and respond to the marketing department with an update on the room rates. All the while, Miles bounces on my chair.

He uses all my tape and an entire pack of post-it notes to make a web. He draws on every single page of a notebook. I could do without that picture staring back at me, but all in all, Miles does an excellent job of staying put. I'm lucky to have such a sweet son, he's the greatest gift in my life.

An alert pops up on my computer screen to remind me of my meeting with my boss Jackson. But as crazy-busy as we are, I suspect he might want to reschedule. He's that kind of boss, realistic and understanding.

"Miles, I'm going to step out and talk to my boss for a minute, and then we'll go see if Ellie is ready for you. Can you hang out here? I'll be right outside that door."

Engrossed in his project, Miles gives me a thumbs up without even turning his head. I quietly step out of my office and leave the door open. Jackson is right there to greet me.

"Hey, crazy day, right?" Jackson runs a hand through his dark hair. "It's slowed down quite a bit on my end for now. We'll meet another time about numbers. But is there anything I can do for you?"

"You aren't supposed to be helping me. If I remember correctly, you're supposed to be leaving early today." I raise an eyebrow at him.

"I am. I'm as good as gone but I don't want to leave you in a bad spot," he says.

"I promise, I've got it. Take the night off. The place won't burn down without you. Besides, aren't there like a dozen other Brewer brothers running around this property if I need them?" I laugh.

"All right. I'm just going to run this luggage up to a guest's room and then I'm leaving."

"You're a lousy bellhop," I smirk. "I'll take the luggage up. You should go and don't call to check in tomorrow either."

"No promises on that one, but thanks. It's room forty-two."

As Jackson turns to leave, I pick up the small luggage. I peek into my office one last time and see that Miles hasn't moved. Then I bolt to the elevator to make the delivery as fast as I can.

AS I COME OUT OF THE elevator and head back toward my office after my impromptu bellhop service. The distinct smell of smoke wafts toward me. At first, I brush it off. But as I pass through the now empty lobby, the smell only gets stronger. My heart rate picks up. By the time I reach the vacant front desk, I know something is on fire and I'm running to my office in a full sprint.

Panic builds in me as I push open the door to my office and a cloud of smoke drifts out. My eyes go wide in shock as I see my son, holding up the plate with the beer cupcake on it. There's a noticeable bite taken out of the side and a candle burning on top of it. Beside it are several burnt matchsticks and the ashes of what I believe used to be a notebook.

"Surprise! Happy birthday, Mom! At first, I didn't know how to light it but I found a video online on your phone and it showed me what to do. It was easy!" He grins and my jaw drops in horror.

"Miles, put that down right now." I hold my hands out and take a cautious step toward him.

"This is how I got it to light up." He holds the matchbook.

"Drop it now." My words come out between clenched teeth.

"Sorry, geez. I just wanted to surprise you, I'm not a baby, I know how to be safe. I'll drop it."

To my horror, Miles drops the entire plate. The rest of the matches in the book erupt into a ball of flames, igniting the paper plate with it.

"Wow," Miles gasps.

Panic whips through me and I look around for something to extinguish the flames. In a moment of desperation, I grab Miles's backpack and throw it on top to smother the flame.

"My backpack!" Miles reaches for the bag and lifts the top portion before I can pull him back. I'm relieved to see the flames are gone, and for a moment my heart rate slows. But the molten mass gives off a black cloud of smoke.

My eyes crawl up the wall in slow motion as I follow the smoke trail to the sprinkler system. I lunge to fan it away but I'm too late. Water rains down on me. I'm horrified as the shrieking bells of the fire alarm echo through my office.

I can hardly breathe as I try to stop it. Then the sound of heavy footsteps stampeding past my door brings more, horrific realizations. *It's not just my office. The entire hotel is hearing the alarm. The alarm system has probably already triggered a call to the fire department. Every guest and employee will be evacuated. We are at capacity.*

"Mom, are you okay? Should we leave?" Miles shouts above the alarm.

"Yes, step right here, get out of the smoke. But also no. Don't leave, it's all right." My words come out in a jumble of stress. "Just sit in that chair behind the counter. I'm going to let everyone know it was a false alarm."

I move into the center of the lobby and wave my hands wildly at the guests flocking out of the stairwell in droves. With my sopping wet hair matted to the side of my face, I must be a sight.

"Go back! It's fine you don't have to leave, it was just an accident there's nothing no problem here! Enjoy your evening at this peaceful resort!" My voice gets more urgent with each person that passes, ignoring me completely.

From there it's a blur. People yelling. People running and pushing to get through the doors. Ellie leaving through the front door hand-in-hand with Miles. Me scrambling in the chaos.

It's ten minutes before I'm standing out front of the empty building with everyone else waiting for the fire engine to arrive and Jackson steps beside me. I explain the whole story, adding an apology after nearly every sentence.

"Well, I have to hand it to you. I thought if you burnt the place down I'd be at least in my truck and off the property by then," Jackson chuckles.

"Very funny." I cut my eyes at him.

"Oh come on, it's not a big deal. You know I'm almost a stepdad now. I understand how these things work. We'll talk to Fire Marshal Dan and he'll give us a warning, then we'll move on with our day. It'll be like none of this ever happened."

"Thanks." My breath comes in short shallow bursts and Jackson's kind words do nothing to calm me as the horrors of what could have happened to my son run rampant in my mind.

Ellie and Miles come to stand beside us but they stay remarkably silent. I wonder if Miles is worried. I wonder how I should handle this as a parent. I brace myself for a solid round of mansplaining from good ole Fire Marshal Dan.

Dan's had his position as the Misty Mountain Fire Marshal for as long as I can remember. He's from a time when men were allowed to talk to women like they are idiots and still hangs his hat on those virtues. I've heard rumors of him retiring, but something tells me he'll be making an appearance today just to add a little salt to the wound. As the fire engine pulls up I exhale and try shaking my nerves out of my hands.

"I already called off my brothers," Jackson says, looking toward the fire truck. "The rest of the resort is back up and running but they have to officially clear the hotel before we can send guests back inside. It's just a formality." Jackson leans in toward me and lowers his voice. "Look, you want me to just talk to Dan for you? I know how he can be."

"No, that's okay. Miles and I need to be accountable for our actions. It's a big deal what happened back there." I swallow hard and look at Miles, but he avoids my gaze, kicking at the gravel on the road.

The door to the engine opens slowly. But to my surprise, the man who steps out looks nothing like old man Dan. This firefighter is young, tall, and ruggedly handsome with bulky muscles and a broad chest. As the man walks toward us, the muscles in my throat tighten and I smooth my, still-wet-from-the-sprinkler, hair behind my ear.

"Uh, Jackson, on second thought, maybe you could just talk to him for me."

Ellie looks at Jackson and shakes her head, scrunching her nose in the center.

Jackson smirks, "Nah, I think you'll be okay. In fact, I'm gonna head home." He jogs away from us and shakes hands with the hot-fire marshal and then points back at Ellie, Miles, and me.

"What was that? Oh no, he's sending him over," I whisper to Ellie and press a hand to my forehead.

"And I'm going to go do... something... reunion-ish. I'll leave you to it. Have a nice chat." Ellie lets go of Miles' hand, and he steps toward me as she disappears into the crowd.

My heart races in my chest as the world's hottest firefighter approaches me. A gentle wind blows and his dark hair dances in it. Meanwhile, I look like my orange tabby after a forced bath. Air bubbles make my stomach gurgle. This must be some kind of cruel birthday joke. *Happy thirty-eighth to me.*

"Are you Emery?"

"I am, hi. This is my son Miles and this whole thing is a misunderstanding. We had a little incident with a candle on a cupcake but there's no problem and I'm sorry you had to waste your time coming out here." I look up at him and a bemused smile tugs at the corner of his mouth.

"I'm Lucas, and I don't mind coming out. It's nice to meet you." He holds out his hand to me and when I place my hand in his, it fits perfectly. The sensation of his skin on mine sends warmth coursing through me and makes my face flush with heat. "And you're Miles?"

"Yes sir, I started a fire," Miles makes his proclamation, and my stomach sinks.

"He did but it was an accident and it was my own fault, I—"

Lucas leans in toward Miles, cutting me off. "You know fire is pretty cool, it's just a matter of learning how to be safe with it. That's the important part. In a minute we'll get the signal from the guys that it's safe to go back inside. Then maybe you can show me what happened."

"Yes I can," Miles says a little too confidently. "I was lighting my mom's matches."

I press my fingertips to my temples. "It isn't what it sounds like, I know better than to let my kid play with matches."

"All good Chief," another firefighter calls out.

"Shall we?" Lucas holds out an arm with a warm smile, and gestures for me to lead the way inside.

"Yes, right." I take a step back toward the hotel and nervous butterflies flap in my stomach.

♥ Read The Hotel at Brew by Brewer today[1] ♥

Thank You

Dear Reader,

Thank you for being here. I am so honored you spent your precious time reading my words. The poorfarm is inspired by a realife brewery where I married my husband over ten years ago. There's something about it that really is magic. If you fell in love at Brew by Brewer too, it would mean the world to me if you left a review. Reviews help other readers find my stories!

Hugs,

Elsie

P.S. I'd love to keep in touch. There are so many more mouthwatering mountain men to come! Use the QR code at the end of this book to sign up for my free newsletter.

About the Author

Elsie James is proud to be a lifelong curvy girl. She writes stories about beautiful, strong, women who always find their happily ever afters. Her books are romantic, sweet, and steamy with a whole lot of heart.

Join my newsletter & get a FREE book![2]

CONNECT WITH ELSIE

Facebook: @authorelsiejames [3]
Instagram: @authorelsiejames[4]
Amazon: amazon.com/author/elsiejames[5]
Email: elsiejames@authorelsiejames.com
Newsletter: https://BookHip.com/RZSKJF[6]

---

2. https://bookhip.com/RZSKJF

3.   https://www.facebook.com/authorelsiejames/

4.   https://www.instagram.com/authorelsiejames/

5.   http://amazon.com/author/elsiejames

6.   https://bookhip.com/RZSKJF

CPSIA information can be obtained
at www.ICGtesting.com
Printed in the USA
JSHW030724110123
36077JS00002B/14